Fetching Love
by
Cassandra Joelle

"Trust in the LORD with all your heart and lean not on your own understanding; in all your ways acknowledge him, and he will make your paths straight."
Proverbs 3:5-6

Table of Contents

Chapter 1
The Purrfect Match
Katie

Walking to work with an engagement ring on feels awkward.

I don't want to assume my co-workers will want to hear about it, so I have decided I will only tell them if they ask. Besides, Jenna already knows, as she was there yesterday when it happened. Yes, this is good; I will be professional and aloof. Mysterious. "Oh, this old thing? Yeah, we're doing the paperwork." In fact, I can't wait to shrug it off so casually to them, so I hope they do ask. I look forward to it! Looking down at my ring again in disbelief...My prayers have been answered, and now, it all makes sense. I am going to spend the rest of my life with Eli.

I can barely contain my excitement, and since I've arrived to work twenty minutes early on this Monday morning, I decide to be useful and set up the conference room for our Monday morning meeting. Because I am so early, swinging by the donut shop wasn't a big deal either. Besides, they were having a sale on my favorite kind. *Buy 1, Pay for 2*, or some kind of steal like that. Honestly, my attention was elsewhere, so when the bill came to $46.75 for a dozen donuts, I swiped my card and left with the warm box.

After grabbing some plates from our office kitchen and a pile of napkins, everything is set up, and I have a few more minutes to spare, so I am brewing a pot of coffee, filling the bubble maker with soapy water, and connecting my phone to the big screen, so it will play the montage of pictures of Eli and me on repeat.

As people start to shuffle in, I do what I knew I would and keep to myself. If it weren't for the donuts having frosted letters on them, spelling out "I SAID YES," they wouldn't have known anything at all is up.

Three Months Later

The attendant at the wedding dress shop assures me that the dress will fit, despite being several —if not a dozen— sizes too large. But once she is done cinching the back, she is right: It fits.

She steps out of the dressing room and gives me a few minutes to take it all in before I show my entourage. It has a beautiful sweetheart neckline with a gorgeous natural waist. There are beautiful beads all over the bodice, big dramatic waves on the skirt, and the attendant tells me I can jazz it up even more with a belt if I want to. All I can picture is a gold buckle that someone would wear to a rodeo, so she slips out and promptly returns with just that. It is a western shop, after all. When I decline, she produces a ribbon that has sparkles on it... "I'd hardly call that a belt."

We both laugh as she agrees that the term is off—it is more of a sash or tie than something made to keep a waistline. It looks beautiful on the dress, but we both agree the dress is better without it. I feel like a bride in this dress.

"I have one more thing I'd like to show you." She disappears out of the satin curtains separating my dressing room from the main floor of the store.

I peek out of the room and savor the experience of being here. Looking around, I wonder why every dressing room couldn't be like those in a bridal store? I imagine bringing my entire entourage with me every time I need a new pair of jeans: *"Okay, ladies. These pants have much larger pockets, since you hated the last ones. I agree with you, mom—I couldn't fit pepper spray in any of those pockets! So, these are not only comfortable, but also quite functional for carrying all the essentials."*

I model the blue jeans with my hands in the front pockets, so everyone can see how roomy they are, doing a full turn, so they can approve of every angle.

"Katie, I hate to say this, as I can tell you like them, but I don't think wide-leg cargo pants are ever going to be in style." Jenna shakes her head profusely. "I can't let you leave with those."

"I have to agree with Jenna, sweetie. Those are a little too, umm. . . baggy for my tastes."

Judy is out, too. That leaves only Samantha, Julie, and my mother.

"I own those in white, and while I can speak for the wonderful functionality, the ten-button fly is a little hard to manage."

My mother has a good point, and I return to the fitting room to try on my next pair: faux-leather corduroys. What could go wrong with these?

The fitting room attendant slips back in, holding the most beautiful applique sash. "This is going to be something." Her eyes are bright with excitement, and I know right away it is just what the dress needs.

It is time for my big reveal.

"You look absolutely beautiful, dear." Judy, my 89-year-old best friend, wipes her eyes with a tissue as my mother passes the box around. Everyone who is near and dear to me is present and teary, for this special occasion is one that I'm not sure would ever come.

My throat lets me know the tears are close behind my eyes. "Thank you," I croak out as I see the reflection of myself in the mirror. A long, ruffled wedding dress skirt billows around the platform I stand on and for the first time in my life, I can see what I look like at average height. The beautiful off-shoulder *sleevelets,* as my mother calls them since they are not quite a sleeve but rather a two-inch strip existing solely to give your arms a toned appearance, are doing their job perfectly. I move to look at the back but am greeted by the unsightly appearance of the twelve clamps that are holding it all together. The boutique owner had sensed this moment and arrives with a long white veil that I already know will be a tripping hazard, but I accept it all the same.

I turn, looking at my mother. She gives me a nod, agreeing with my eyes that this dress is it.

"This is the dress!" My mother jumps up, putting her hands in the prayer position and lets out a holler, "Thank you, Jesus! My daughter has found a husband!" I give her a sideways look, and she immediately corrects herself. "A dress. She's found THE DRESS!" All the ladies clap and suddenly, my mother is holding an old-fashioned camcorder.

"Mom? Where did that come—".

She cuts me off. "Katie, say hi to your Aunt Penny and Uncle Don, who don't have internet and still have a VCR."

"I hope they also don't have their hearing," Judy replies.

"H-hi guys, um. . .this isn't quite the moment I'd planned on sharing since it's not my size, but this is the dress I just picked out." I smile awkwardly, showing all my teeth in the process.

My mother turns the camcorder to herself. "As promised, I'm investigating—I mean, *documenting* every detail of Katie's wedding *evidence,* because I know you two didn't believe me when I called last fall to tell you the news of her engagement." She turns the camera back to me. "This may be circumstantial and won't hold up in court—*since anyone these days can go buy a wedding dress,* —but believe it. My daughter is getting married!"

We all look on to my mother in wonder as she zooms in on my left hand. "Exhibit A: Katie is wearing an engagement ring."

My ears perk up at Judy and Julie's conversation. "A little, I'm afraid. I am not sure exactly *which* personality disorders, but I do know it's at least two of them."

"Mom, can we do this later? I can send them a copy of our marriage license if that helps?" I burst out laughing, as it sounds even more ridiculous than it does in my head that relatives I hardly know want *proof.*

She nods and turns off the camera. "This thing is just so dang heavy anyway. Oh, and I just remembered; I forgot to put the tape in! I had to order that off eBay; stores don't even sell them anymore."

"Okay, that's good. I'd rather wait until I have a film-worthy moment before showing anyone anything. Why do they not believe I'm getting married?"

"Nothing personal, Katie. You know how they don't trust the phone ever since they got that prank phone call saying they'd won a lifetime supply of pizza. Now, they just assume all the BEST news isn't real!"

I am relieved it had nothing to do with myself and vow to send them a wedding photo with a pizza gift card.

"Eli is going to love you in that dress!" Julie says to change the subject, and everyone eagerly agrees.

"Oh, I can't wait to see the look on his face when he sees his beautiful bride!"

"Hope her mom has the camera ready for that one."

"He's going to go crazy when he sees you!"

The shop attendant brings over various other accessories for me to try, including a different veil that is shorter. What I don't *love* is that it is attached to a white cowboy hat.

"I'm just not sure it's my look." I gaze at the large hat on my head, while seeing the reflection of my loved ones stifling laughter. "I think I'll stick to the traditional look." I break out into a laugh along with everyone else.

"I kind of like it," Julie snickers as I toss the hat to her. She puts it on, and we are all impressed with how natural it looks.

"There are few people who can pull that off, Julie, and you are one of them. I have the same luck with sombreros." My mother analyzes it out loud.

We look at my mother with laughter while the attendant tries on another veil. It has a shimmer to it, along with small purple flowers at the end. I absolutely love it.

"What are your colors, Katie?" the attendant, Rachel, asks.

"We don't really have colors, as it's at our church, and it's not going to be decorated head to toe, but we like the colors of spring. Judy is bringing fresh flowers from her garden and just so happens to have hyacinth and lilacs, which will be perfect with this veil."

Judy smiles as my mother thanks her profusely for the flowers.

"That was so generous of you, Judy! When I sent you the bulbs last fall, I hope you didn't feel like that's what I wanted you to do. Katie just said how much you enjoyed getting out in your garden."

"I know, dear. When you sent them for my birthday, I just had an inkling that this might happen soon, and if it worked out, how great would that be? It means the world to me that I can provide something for my sweet Katie's big day. And you don't have to thank me again. You already went above and beyond by sending me that popcorn bouquet. Oh, the dental bills that followed, though. At my age, I'm towing the line just to keep my teeth. Whenever I go in, I think they are going to bring out the pliers. Thankfully, I managed to get out of there intact once again. They have banned me from eating it, however."

My mother consoles Judy from being banned from everyone's favorite snack as Jenna suggests we switch things up by eating rice cakes instead. Oh, the groans that follow.

"I don't mind a little danger in my food, Jenna. If I wanted to eat Styrofoam, I'd skip the pretense and do so."

Rachel brings out the same sash I am already wearing, but in lavender. I gasp when I see that it matches the veil. I think it is beautiful. Turning back to my group to get their opinion, I see that someone has clipped a small veil into my miniature poodle Dolly's hair when I had my back turned. We all start giggling uncontrollably at the sight, as Dolly looks pleased to receive the attention while she sits on Judy's lap.

"I don't think she could get any cuter!" I shout out.

Judy giggles and refocuses back to the task at hand.

"The belt is stunning, Katie. It really brings it all together." Judy beams.

Everyone is quick to agree, including my mother. I absolutely love it. My mother audibly gasps, and we all turn to her.

"Katie. . ." She has her hand over her mouth. "Your grandma's amethyst earrings!"

I return her gasp when I remember the stunning pair of sparkling purple studs that my late grandma Pathy left my mom when she passed. "I can't think of anything more fitting for this gown! May I borrow them?"   My mother is already nodding as she wipes the tears from her eyes. "There's no better way to honor Grandma Pathy. I'll have your father bring them."

"Did you say Kathy?" Judy asks my mother. "I'm a little hard of hearing these days, but I want to get it right."

My mother nods and laughs. "Well, her first name is Kathy, but my father, her husband, was Pat. We always referred to them as Pat and Kathy, until one day, I transposed the letters, and it was Kat and Pathy. It's kind of just stuck, and we just called her Pathy ever since."   I recall my grandparents lovingly before Jenna changes the subject.

"Tell us about your honeymoon, Katie," Jenna prompts me, and I steps off the platform and feel the dress sway as I talk.

"We are going on a ski trip in Alaska," I gush. "It's always been his dream to travel to the winter wonderland, and he thought our honeymoon would be the perfect time to see it."

"That sounds incredible! I did a cruise once with my parents to Southeast Alaska in the summertime. Talk about heaven on earth!" Samantha beams.

"How fun is that? I know Eli considered us going on a cruise, but after that experience my mom had, I'm not sure if I have it in me."

"What experience did I have, Katie?"

I pull back my chin in surprise. "Umm...When you contracted that horrible virus from the buffet on the second day of your trip, they locked you in your room for the remainder of the 14-day cruise. You don't remember?"

She nods in recollection.

"Anyway, I think Alaska is the perfect place for a romantic honeymoon," Samantha adds, thankfully changing the subject.

"Look at her; she's positively bedazzled in love," Judy tells the other ladies. "I am so happy for you, Katie."

"Thank you, Judy. And thank you all for being here for me today. Mom, thank you for flying in for the month, even though it will be over in a few weeks, and for offering to pet sit during our honeymoon. Jenna, thank you for picking up the slack at work, so I can take all this time off. And Judy, Samantha, and Julie, thank you for helping plan our wedding at such short notice. I know it was a little strenuous to have it such a short time later, but we are just so excited to start our lives together. . .finally."

Cordial clapping ensues, and I feel a wave of dizziness hit as I start to lose my footing. After unsuccessfully trying to catch myself and finding nothing to hold on to, my foot catches under the front of the dress, and I slowly tumble to the floor, landing on my side.

"Katie! Are you okay?" Jenna is the first to my side as I hold my hand to my head.

I am okay, just a little embarrassed. "Yes . . . I am not sure what that was. I feel a little light-headed is all..."

She helps me off the pedestal, as my mother helps me sit down in a white upholstered chair.

"Have you eaten today, Katie?" My mother pulls a digital thermometer out of her purse and starts taking my temperature. "You are a perfect ninety-six degrees, so it's not the flu."

"I should hope not." I stifle a laugh, lightening the mood. "I'm okay, but you're right; I think I must be famished." I've been trying to be good diet-wise, so I could fit into a dress, having only a piece of toast this morning. Little do I know it's all rope and jumper cables in the back. I stand back up, the dizzy spell having passed, and consider doing a twirl for my audience, but I don't want to push it.

The boutique manager of *The Hitching Post* waltzes over, still wearing the measuring tape on her shoulders like a scarf.

"I have excellent news, Katie! While we specialize in short-term planning, I am extremely excited to tell you I can have this dress in your size in three days!"

We all cheer.

"What is the date of your wedding?"

My head is spinning from my fall, but I am hoping no one tells the manager, as I don't want to make any more of a fuss. I'm sure I am fine, but the shock hasn't left my cheeks yet as I feel unusually flushed.

"March 11th. Just a few weeks from today," Judy squeals, as she pops a bottle of sparkling cider, and the group cheers with her.

The manager raises her eyebrows at my date, prompting an explanation.

"I wanted to wait until everyone was with me to go shopping, including my mom from out of state, even though that might mean I get something off the rack, with it cutting it so close, and all."

"Well, we are certainly cutting it close, but that's why *The Hitching Post* is the best in the business! That's going to be perfect, Katie. What's the *future last name* I can put it under?"

My cheeks redden with excitement. "Skatey."

The woman has a puzzled look on her face for a moment, then subsides into a laugh. "That's just. . .darling, isn't it?"

"Katie! Skatey! Katie! Skatey!" My group of supporters has clearly let the fizzy, sugary bubbles cut off their air supply as the chant becomes contagious.

"Thank you for getting that so quickly for us." My mother shakes the hand of the manager and turns back to our group. "Okay, ladies. My Katie needs to eat. Who's hungry? Shall we take this party to the Olive Pit?" my mother shouts out over the joyous chants, and everyone agrees and starts gathering up their belongings. My mom follows me into the fitting room, so she can remove the clamps. "Are you sure you are okay, Katie? What was that fall about? I know you've inherited my clumsy genetics, but it came out of nowhere." "Honestly, I have no idea. That's never happened before."

My mother goes silent in her concern, and my stomach does a flip in reaction to the nerves. "It kind of reminded me of the time you slid *under* the Christmas tree."

I let out a laugh and eventually, my mother nods and smiles, but there is a hesitancy to her.

"If it happens again, I think it would be wise to see a doctor, that's all."

I know my mother is right, and I agree with her and move the conversation along, as she is down to the last clamp. "Do you really think this dress is the one? I mean, I do, but out of all of them, did it look the best on me?" I ask her.

She is already nodding in overwhelming agreement.

"Oh yes! Katie—you know I wouldn't lie to you—except that one time because you just so desperately wanted those pleather pants, even though I knew the zipper would bust because of your. . . *proportions* —you can trust me. This dress looks like it was made for you. Let me put it this way: *I wouldn't want you wearing it in an alley late at night.*"

In my mother's own way, this is the highest compliment achievable. I am so pleased that she approves of the dress as much as I do and now it is time to spend the rest of the day with all the ladies who have come to celebrate with me.

The dress is heavy fabric, but I attribute much of the weight to the metal clamps that have been keeping it on my body. Still, the last time I was wearing this many layers was in middle school when it was no longer acceptable to wear *just one polo shirt,* or *just one belt;* you had to wear several of each item. I'm not sure where that trend originated or ended, but I remember it being a very dark time, as I only owned one Newsboy style hat and after a long, distressing day at the mini-mall, I couldn't find another that would fashionably lay atop it.

Thankfully, butterfly hair clips were starting to make their rounds, and I found solace in twisting dozens of crispy, orange, home-bleached hair strands into the colorful bug clips. As I waltzed into the cafeteria the next day wearing my two polo shirts with popped collars on each, three woven chokers, five metallic belts in all the colors of the rainbow, and my seventeen butterfly clips, instead of the cheers I was expecting from my *table* (a ragtag bunch of kids who didn't have anywhere else to sit), they looked at me in shame.

"That's out." One of the girls pointed at my entire look. "Liquid leather is in."

I did the only thing one could do when they went to school and realized the risky outfit they were *feeling* in the morning wasn't so cute after all. The last time I appeared in the nurse's office, I said I wasn't well and that my mother immediately needed to be summoned to take me home at once. Then, I asked if I could wait it out in the meantime with her. I was wearing plaid pants, high-heeled clogs and two awful pig tails But not just any pigtails: The kind with a horrible—no, *horrendous*— back part that you could only achieve if you were drunk, armless, or temporarily blinded from staring into a strobe light for too long. I was only twelve and was none of those things, so it was all on me. The nurse once again took one look at me and nodded, reaching for her phone directory while stifling back a laugh.

My mother starts unclamping the last piece of hardware while holding the dress on. "I should ask to buy some of these in case we need to jump your car. I'd hate to have you stranded somewhere at night."

"Good thing I don't go out at night. Besides, in a few weeks, I'll have a husband who can come to my rescue."

My mother smiles and nods. We are all head over heels for Eli.

"Have you investigated the adoption paperwork for Eli to become Dolly's legal secondary guardian?"

I let out a snort laugh. "I don't think that's how it works."

"You better believe that's how it works, Katie. Add him to everything in case you get struck by lightning and next thing you know, *Dolly becomes a ward of the courts*."

"Does the television ever actually *turn off* in your house? Or do you come up with this stuff on your own?"

She finally removes the last clamp, and the dress triples in size, falling off me like a rock from the sky, almost taking my slip with it from the force.   "Fine, don't listen to me. I'll be right there when you wake up from a coma and tell you that Dolly's been through *probate*. We can only pray the court has their wits about them to at least assign me temporary custody."

I shoot her a look meaning, *Can we not?*   "Okay, okay. Don't be so touchy; you know I'm right, but we will leave it at that."

She laughs and leaves the dressing room. I change back into my dark jeans, black boots, and green top, the outfit that Eli has said is his favorite. Slipping the *Bride to Be* sash over my head, I take a long glance at myself in the mirror and feel a surge of excitement.

"Dear Jesus,
I can't believe the joy I feel.
Thank You from every fiber of my being for the gifts You have given me.
You have once again shown the power and wisdom of Your timing, which is perfect, every time.
I pray that my fall was just a freak anomaly, and my health is okay.

In Your name,
Amen."

I can see the hustle and bustle of my mother and the rest who have become like family to me as I get ready to leave, since the dressing room curtain isn't wide enough to provide privacy, as they never are.

I feel the overpowering peace of Jesus wash over me. *I will trust in Him and not think again of my fall.* Tearing the curtain open, I feel the adrenaline pump through my veins.

"Who's ready to eat? Because I have room to spare in that dress!"

On our way out, we pass the accessories that Rachel has been sourcing from. There are cowboy hats in every color: some with veils, some with bling, and hat bands with veils, so you can customize any look. There is also a wide selection of cowboy boots, bedazzled stick horses, and bouquet wraps. I am reading the size guide for the garter belts with shotgun shells when I see the rest of my group move on to a wall dedicated to pet accessories that I didn't see when we walked in.

Jenna waves me over. "Katie, you need to come see this right away." Everyone gathers, and we are quickly in love with all the offerings. I tell the manager we will be taking the miniature veil for Dolly, as well as the small white bowtie for Carter.

"I wonder if you could sell your creations here, Katie?"

It is true that I have been making little dog dresses ever since that first week I got Dolly, and I'm not even sure how it happened, but one day after posting a photo of one on my social media, a friend shared it, and next thing I knew, a costume boutique owner named Trisha Pawsbury had messaged me that her costume store would love to carry some dog clothes. Now, I am sending her a small collection of one-of-a-kind pieces every month that I make in my spare time. Sometimes, they are cohesive to each other; sometimes, they are as random as a passing car. I get sixty percent of the profits, so this extra money I've been making goes into Dolly's teeth cleaning fund. Who knew how expensive cleaning a small dog's micro teeth would be?

If I had been asked before I had a pet what I thought a dental treatment might cost, I would have first questioned the validity of the procedure. Dogs have been our companions for thousands of years. Who decided they needed dental visits? I wonder if similar things happen when a dog goes in:

"Katie Fitzgerald?" I stand up when the veterinarian calls my name and go forward.

"How did Dolly do?" As I ask, the veterinarian smiles.

"She did great! She's just waking up, so still a little groggy. I'm afraid we were a bit too late on the teeth cleaning."

"Oh no, what does that mean?" Images of my Dolly coming out toothless pop into my head.

"She had two cavities that we filled, and we found evidence of a little teeth grinding. But don't worry, we've fit her for a custom night guard."

Trisha said she started her boutique intending to sell pet costumes only, but it was in a time when dressing up your pet wasn't as mainstream or accepted. Nowadays, dogs have wardrobes that compete with our own, so she's ready to expand again into the doggy fashion world.

Trisha goes by the namesake store name "Trisha Pawsbury," and while I'm not sure if that's her legal name, I love it. She hopes that I expand into pet costuming so that I can keep up with the demand from her customers.

While I was flattered that she was interested in anything I sent her, I didn't have the capability or desire to make the elaborate kinds of costumes she's looking for, so she has been pleased enough with what I can send her in a month. But as time has gone on, I have felt my abilities grow, and in this last shipment, I included a small collection of headwear in oversized bows with elastic hats fashioned from doll accessories, and even a small wig that had mermaid shells attached.

I just mailed it out a few days ago, so I am expecting an email from Trisha soon with her thoughts. I am confident she will love them. And I had just wrapped up the forming of my new LLC, *Pawsh,* thanks to Darren at work, who filed it for me in exchange for a set of bandanas and hair bows for his dog, Lulu. For the tip, I threw in some beaded collars and a sock set that I bought for Dolly but never ended up using.

Darren and his wife, Lucy, had adopted little Lulu after the mad rush of everyone else adopting. Darren explained, one Monday morning at our new weekly "dish" session, where we could optionally share things about our lives, that he felt inspired to get a pet right away just like everyone else. But first, he wanted to talk things over with Lucy and line up care beforehand for the pet while they travel. I found that very admirable since I hadn't even considered it. Luckily, Darren's parents were able to come to America and get visas, so Darren said he and his wife have become full-time babysitters, so it takes the pressure off the baby discussions for a while. Double win.

Back to reality, I love all of the pet accessories at *The Hitching Post.*

"Is Dolly going to be coming to the wedding? I know you'd want both dogs to be there. Dolly and Carter are welcome at Three Maples anytime!" Julie says, breaking me out of my thoughts of work, with an expectant smile.

"Of course! I don't know the logistics, but we thought she would be the flower girl and Carter the ring bearer. He's already proven his skills!" I blush again at the memory of Eli proposing a few weeks ago, with Carter helping, and feel the weight of the ring on my finger.

"What a darling idea. Carter is such a handsome little guy!" Judy beams.

"They both are," I gush, and everyone *oohs and awes.*

After settling the payment details with Rachel, I am ready to leave.

"Did I overhear that you make pet accessories?" Rachel asks.

"I make dog clothes, mostly dresses but also some bandanas, and I'm exploring headwear."

Rachel's eyes widen with excitement, and she claps. "That is JUST what our little cowpokes need down here! Have you ever created western wear? I'd be in the market to carry some products if they had fringe, tassels, paisley, or even better—all the above!"

In fact, after seeing all these western creations, I have just the creation in mind for her store, but I'm not sure what she will think of it.   "What about doggy chaps? I have these little strips of faux leather left over from a purse repair and—". Rachel cuts me off.

"Yes! Make them sequined, and I'll pay extra!" She pulls out her business card and writes her personal cell phone number on the back. "Here—I am the co-owner of the shop, and I also manage it. My sister is the other owner, and just so you are aware, we are twins. People get us confused all the time. It doesn't help that her name is Raquel." She throws her arms up, laughing, "I don't get it either."

We agree that I will send her a picture with a creation when I have something ready to show, but with my wedding, honeymoon, and the fact that Eli and I will need to find something bigger than our identical apartments filled with our own stuff, it is going to be a few months.

She is happy with that timeline. "There's no rush at all, Katie. This is a wedding boutique, and weddings happen all year long. We also have wedding guests come in looking for things to wear to the weddings, you see; hence, the reason I think the chaps will do so well. In fact, I just had a Chihuahua in here last month who could've really used a pair for his parents' wedding. They got married on horseback. Little guy was just wearing Wranglers and a button up."

My mother enters the chat. "Katie, you should add a hook for rope on those chaps. I'm sure there are a lot of poodles, Yorkies, and Chihuahuas that also have the consideration of steer roping."

We take three separate cars to the Olive Pit, with me riding alone with my mother who drives.

"This rental is so nice. You may need to look into something larger like this, Katie. You're about to be a family of four."

"According to portion sizes, I've always been a family of four." I point it out to her.

She doesn't miss a beat. "You are going to need something safe and comfortable. What kind of car seat does Carter use? Both dogs will need a permanent setup. Maybe that's something I can investigate while you're on your honeymoon." She beams with excitement as she is the one who gets to watch the dogs while we are away.

"Sure, I mean, it wouldn't hurt for us to consider it, but it will have to be something Eli and I figure out, of course." I am so excited to make joint decisions with my future husband.

"Of course, Katie. And while we are talking about your honeymoon, know that you can always get daily check-ins from the dogs via text, but try to let go and relax. I know you both will be missing them like crazy, but don't worry—I'll take such good care of them; they won't even have a second to themselves to miss you. I just want you two to have fun and not worry about anything."

"Thank you for doing that. What about Edward? Will he miss you?"

"You know how he is with your dad. They enjoy their time together... Your dad is referring to the time as his *vacation.*"

Laughing, I thank her, and she makes a sharp turn, coming to a screeching halt in the Olive Pit parking lot.

"Breadsticks, here we come!"

I feel a sudden wave of dizziness come back over me, but my mother is already out of her seat and shutting the door behind her. I wait just a moment, putting my head down as if I am tying my shoes, and it passes as quickly as it came. "I really need to eat," I whisper.

We spend the rest of the afternoon enjoying each other's company over bowls of warm pasta, dessert, pitchers of lemonade, and chocolate lava cake. I am feeling more energetic as I drink glasses of iced tea and thankfully, my vision remains clear. My pants feel like they are about to burst open at the button when I finally call it.   "I know my dress has room to spare, but I might need it taken out if I have another bite, so now seems like the perfect time to ask you all to be my bridesmaids?"

The ladies gasp and one by one, agree, my mother being the last.

"Who is going to film it if I'm your maid of honor?"

I laugh but also consider the point.

"I've just gotten the camcorder and everything. As much as I want to be standing up there with you, I'd much rather get the evidence—I mean, the video proof of the big day. It is part of my gift to you and Eli."

I agree with her on that. "Yes, you're right, and thank you, mom, for doing that. It's so thoughtful of you and a memory we can cherish for decades to come. And I'm sure the camcorder wasn't cheap, considering it's a relic and all."

My mother nods, smiling.

"I'm happy to do it. I've found it's quite handy to have. And there's a store back home that will convert VHS to DVD to MP4, so I can share videos with the internet. Why, it's so easy to do these days. I'm starting to wonder why I even have a smartphone that fits in my pocket when I can just as easily haul this heavy machine, take a trip down to the electronic gurus, wait 5-7 business days, and have it all the same."

I look into her eyes to see if she is joking, but she isn't,' everyone else stifles back their laughter.

"I just have to figure out how to get music from my iPod to be on the videotapes."

My eyes widen. I had not seen an iPod in years. Suddenly, my knees start to hurt, my sciatica is acting up, and I remember it is time for my Metamucil.

Samantha's phone is sitting on the table chimes, and my eyes catch hers. "Okay, enough about the wedding—Samantha, it's your turn to spill about your new romance with Mitchell!"

Samantha puts her hands over her face as she sheepishly tries to hide her blushing, and everyone starts egging her on.

"Oh yes, that new handsome boy at church you've been bringing along. What's the situation, dear?" Judy asks, as she twirls pasta onto her fork.

"Well, I didn't want to take away from your day, Katie. . ." Samantha's eyes get wide, and she looks nervous. "But if you really want to know. . ."

Everyone, including myself, begs her for more information.

"Last night he asked me a really important question!"

Everyone gasps at the table, and Judy starts to tear up as my mother leans over and asks in a hushed tone, "He wants you to be his alibi?"

Samantha stares back at her for a minute before busting up laughing., Soon, the rest of the table joins in.

"He asked me to be his girlfriend! We are officially dating now. And he gave me something."

"Samantha—do tell us the details. I could not be any happier for you both!"

Samantha hesitates for a moment and then nods as she reaches for the necklace she's wearing that's tucked into her shirt. She pulls it out, revealing a beautiful gold ring with a small pink stone. I cheer with joy for the woman who has become my dear friend—who inadvertently changed my life for the better the day she decided to speak at our church about her full animal shelter. Had she not parked next to me, or had she left right after her speech, or had the Lord not put in her heart to do that work in the first place… Why, I couldn't imagine what my life would be like right now. I'm guessing more of the same loneliness and waiting.

Not a day goes by that I don't sit in awe of God's plan for my life and revel at this brilliant interwoven path that I didn't see coming. And I couldn't think of a better outcome for my life if I tried.

Katie's Biblical Application
"For I know the plans I have for you," declares the Lord, "plans to prosper you and not to harm you, plans to give you hope and a future." —Jeremiah 29:11

"Thank you, Katie, for putting the bug in my ear that my perfect man was out there, working at PetWorld!" Samantha starts laughing and explains her ring. "I know we are a little old for promise rings, but it's important to Mitchell and I that we do this right. This little ring means we see a future together and will save ourselves for marriage—even if that hasn't always been the case in either of our lives." Samantha looks up and only sees supportive faces. "Because, well. . . we've all made mistakes, but..." Samantha freezes mid-sentence.

Jenna puts her arm around her. "We all fall short of the glory of God. Mistakes? I've made *millions.* And still do. But we can come back from it. God has cleansed you both white as snow, and I'm so proud of you for this commitment you've made to one another."

Watching Jenna's growing faith over the last few months has been beautiful. Samantha hugs her.

Judy beams. "It's a lovely ring, sweetheart. And he's one dapper fellow. Katie tells me he also has four Pomeranians, just like you? And to think I even encouraged Katie to go line-dancing to meet a man, when all she had to do was go to the animal shelter!"

Everyone roars and starts talking about their pets, thanks to Samantha.

"Samantha, you have changed all of our lives with your work. If it wasn't for you, none of us would be here right now."

As I speak, a small giggle comes out from my mother who is holding her camcorder again as she zooms in on the ring Samantha is holding.

"Are you sure about that, Katie? You loved coming here for the all-you-can-eat pasta bowls when you were single, too."

It's a good thing my mother doesn't have the camcorder pointed to me as I give her a look like, *Really?*

Everyone is still giggling while I tell Samantha to put the ring on her finger. "There's nothing more I could ask for than for you to wear your new ring, Samantha!"

"Thank you, Katie! I just didn't want you to feel like this wasn't your day."

"Now, it's even more special for me, and all of us get to share this together!"

"Speaking of dogs. . ." Jenna asks Samantha how well her Pomeranians get along with Mitchell's brood. "Have they shown any signs of being territorial?"

Samantha finishes chewing a bite of her pasta primavera and shakes her head. "Thankfully, no. The Pomeranians have a little circus going on whenever they see each other. It's like they are long lost siblings or something."

"Wouldn't that be bizarre if they were?" My mother, now without the camcorder, has her head leaning on her hand and is completely invested in the conversation.

I laugh, considering that's exactly what happened to me with Eli, having surmised our dogs were siblings and all.

"Stranger things have happened, haven't they, Katie?" Samantha winks at me. "Yes, the Poms are fine, thankfully. But then

I have the two Chihuahua mixes, but those have been in kind of a 'fostering' situation. I mean, technically, yes; they are foster dogs, as I was at capacity when they came into the shelter, and they were desperate for decompression time and socialization, so I brought them home. They are really thriving now. It's been about four months, and even though it's just been word of mouth, I've already had three people contact me to meet them."

"That's wonderful, Samantha. You're making a huge difference." Judy beams.

Samantha thanks her. "I just am having trouble letting them go... I do not want them to feel like they were given up again."

Everyone chimes in, encouraging her to feel better about it.

"Fostering is rewarding because you change an outcome and give a family a happier dog that's ready for love, but it's scary, too, because they've added so much to my life; I don't want to lose that."

Everyone chimes in and comforts Samantha, including my mother, who recounts when she lost Bubba.

"I thought my life was over. One minute, I was pushing him in a stroller at the mall, browsing the clearance racks at Forever 21. Katie, do you remember that time you got stuck in a zipper in their fitting room? They had to come in with scissors and cut you out of that sequined jumpsuit. Anyway, the next thing I know, Bubba is gone. He must have caught eyes with the flip-flop wall at Old Navy across the hall and jumped out when I wasn't looking. Only after a two-hour security lockdown was he finally found, but he'd already destroyed three pairs of those things. I had to buy them all. One pair was still wearable, but of course he had to chew ones that weren't my size. Still, I kept them because his teeth marks were just so cute."

"Anyway," I choke out through the laughter at the story, "there's no rush to find them homes if you're not ready, right?"

Samantha shrugs. "Well, I suppose not, but I feel like the longer I wait, the harder it's going to be on all of us. I just want to find the right family. I would never forgive myself if they went to the wrong people."

"Exactly. You don't want to accidentally click onto the classifieds page and see that the new owners are selling pictures of their feet. I get it."

My mother knows all too much about screening people, and suddenly, I come up with a solution.

"I have an idea! What if my mother helps you make the selection? She can perform mobile background checks and everything!"

My mother loves the idea.

"It's true, Samantha. I even have a professional stylus pen that they can sign their names with and submit to my investigation. It's all legit."

Samantha agrees to it joyfully.

"I love that idea! Thank you, ladies. I came here today with a heaviness I didn't realize about finding the perfect home for these two little dogs that I love so much, and now that weight has been lifted."

The waiter comes and drops the bill on the table, and my mother snatches it up with a speed reserved for a cheetah. "I got it, ladies. Thank you all again for being here with us today. You sure know how to make a mother feel special—that her daughter is so loved."

"Thanks, mom." I give her a hug, and we shuffle out of the booth while everyone else thanks her. Then, we say our goodbyes.

"Want to get together again this week? I would love to see you once more before things get too crazy," Samantha says as she hugs me goodbye.

"I would love to do that! Yes, anytime. And we are available to review your potential adopters. That's important to me, too."

I beam with joy as we make plans for a relaxing meetup in the coming days, and I know my mother will be jumping for joy that she has new people to investigate.

Chapter 2
Let The Fur Fly
Samantha

My heart leaps at the thought of Mitchell. It isn't just his boyish looks or the thought of kissing his pillowy lips; it is his personality as well. I can't deny the attraction I feel to him is strong—like, *borderline improper* strong; there is no doubt a little bit of the "L" word is going on here. Just the thought of his arms around me makes me blush, but there is something else going on here, too.

God knows my struggles, but so does the enemy. I'm not saying that I think the devil made Mitchell so dang attractive to me, but my temptation surrounding him is *off the charts.* Surely, I hope to marry a man that I feel strongly about, but there's something about these feelings that reminds me of my forgiven sins in a way that I don't like. Yes, I have a past, but I've become a born-again

Christian and have been washed clean. I am living through the Lord's grace and it's freeing. So why is it that I feel like I am heading in the wrong direction?

When I met Mitchell, it felt like a lightbulb turned on in my brain and cast a renewed awareness into all the wrong turns I've made in my life. Here was this guy that checked all my boxes on physical appearance, loves dogs in the same way I do, and is a believer. I just assumed the relationship was from God.

I've been very honest with him about my past. He says he does not judge me and instead, treats me with a level of respect I have never received from a man before. That being said, Mitchell's squeaky-clean past consists of one or two relationships scattered over years of time, and since none of them were with women like I used to be, he doesn't have his guard up as much as I wish he would. For instance, we went and saw a movie last week. We were some of the only ones in the movie theater, and my legs just guided us to the back row. Why did I do that? When I realized what I was doing, I turned around and led us to the front row. Mitchell took it in stride, even though we both had an uncomfortable bend in our necks watching that close.

After the movie, I explained to Mitchell about the struggles I was facing with temptation and overall feelings of lust. At first, he thought I was flattering him and was nonchalant, but after some time, he too felt the weight of the problem, and we agreed we would try harder to not let ourselves be in those situations. And then he brought up the "M" word. Yep, marriage. He told me he doesn't date just for fun, and that he wouldn't be with me unless he felt something serious could come of it. I happily agreed with him, feeling the same, but that's when I had that thing happen where you get a weird feeling in your gut. Or like when you minorly electrocute yourself plugging in a thrift store appliance; you feel the sudden shock, worry sets in and you're thankful that you didn't die, all at the same time. You'd think hearing those words from my dreamboat boyfriend would make me feel like I was on cloud 9, not like I just got whiplashed from a shoddy throwback blender. *No, no. Don't use that to make our milkshakes, it's just for looks.*

The more I thought of what Mitchell said, I realized he meant his words wholly because truthfully, he's never dated. His two relationships were short-lived and years apart. From what I've gathered from his recounting of them and the few hours I spent social media sleuthing, they were instigated by the woman and also ended by the woman after a few short weeks. At first, I felt relieved that he had no skeletons in his closet and those women didn't snatch him up immediately like I did. I felt that he had been preserved for me in a way. But Mitchell was different from the other men I've dated, wanted to date, or even thought about dating. He didn't seem to have any desire whatsoever for a physical relationship. When I asked him about it, I expected him to say that he was waiting for marriage. But it wasn't even on his radar. He would simply shrug it off and say he's never really thought about it. *Really?*

There are two possible outcomes in this scenario: Mitchell hasn't found the right woman that lights his heart on fire with desire, or he is not burning with passion for anyone and making decisions for his future based on his mind. It's hard to dismiss him for that. Our lives do fit together so well... But I must admit, I would like him to want to kiss me. Or even give me a deep hug. Everything now feels so... platonic. I hate to dwell on the issue, but it makes me feel like he's not attracted to me or interested in anything more than a friendship, and I'm feeling this still despite the new ring on my finger.

Last night, Mitchell called and invited me out to ice cream. I hadn't seen him or stopped praying since the movie theater incident, so I said yes, considering it was within our boundaries of a public place and surely, I wasn't going to want to stick my tongue down his throat at a family ice cream parlor. And that's when he really surprised me with this promise ring.

"Samantha, I know it's still early in our relationship, but I've given it a lot of thought, and this does seem like the real deal. I don't want to put any unnecessary pressure on us, but I would like to give you this ring in commitment to our relationship abstaining from physical acts until if... or *when* we marry."

My cheeks went red, but it didn't start or stop at my face. It was the deep, radiating heat that started in my gut and went outward. I had so many questions; for one, if we did get married, would a switch be flipped and suddenly he would be burning with passion like myself? Or am I going down a darkened road that is going to leave me feeling unwanted, unloved and lonely in the end? Despite these feelings, I did what I thought was right, even just for now, and accepted the ring.

I was elated at the symbolic gesture of the ring and admired the beautiful pink stone set into the rose metal. He explained he'd found it at an antique shop years ago, and though he was single at the time, knew the ring would have a special purpose in his life one day. Watching his beautiful face explain the gift, I thought of how much I longed for him to embrace me. I took a breath and excused myself to the ladies' room, citing the sticky table from the ice cream remnants were making my hands feel gross, and I didn't want to get anything on the ring. Mitchell beamed, feeling proud of the jewelry on my hand as I walked away.

After washing up, I splashed some cool water on my face and neck and gaped at my reflection. I looked as good as I was capable of, my blonde bob styled straight and not a strand out of place. My crisp blue eyes looked even brighter with my jet black eyeliner winged out on my eyelids, and I wore a light shimmer shadow on the lid. This was my "date night" look, designed to entice and give me a mystique. I let out my breath and sighed. I started praying under my breath. "Lord, when I chose to follow you, I committed to denying myself. I am deeply struggling with temptation and doubt. Please light my path, God. If Mitchell is not the one, or if I am not ready for what's to come, I pray that you make it clear and slam this door shut. Amen." I closed my eyes as I stood in silence, feeling the water from the faucet pour over my hands as I reflected on my prayer.

The bathroom door swung open with such force, I nearly slipped and fell from the fright. I was surprised to see it was a small child whose arms were entirely covered in ice cream.

"Wash up, Sylvie." Her mom was quickly behind her.

I watched the child step onto a small stool to raise herself enough to reach the sink. She's done this before. I stole a glance at her mother while I finished the facade of washing my hands. The mother was encouraging her beautiful daughter to use enough soap, and to get all the ice cream washed off. For some reason, I was in a trance watching these two.

"Someone's having fun." I casually referenced the girl as I grabbed two sheets of paper towels to dry my hands, taking my sweet time.

"Oh yes. It's miss Sylvie's fourth birthday, and that meant an extra scoop of her favorite ice cream."

I looked back at the sweet daughter who was wearing an oversized bright pink hair bow that had little sparkles in it that matched the pink bell bottoms she wore. Her white shirt was more like a smock, chosen for the clothing protection quality no doubt.

"And what is your favorite ice cream, Sylvie?"

"Bubblegum with sprinkles." She playfully stuck out her tongue to show me its blue color and giggled her way into a fit.

"Oh, to be young." Her mother laughed and helped her daughter off the stool, drying her hands and they returned to the parlor.

What had just happened? I was feeling something... new, and it wasn't the ring Mitchell had just put on my finger.

Chapter 3
Sit, Stay, Love
Katie

Now that we have returned from the Olive Pit, my mother tidies up my living room and fluffs up the couch pillows.

"I'm sorry I got rid of the pullout now. I hope you don't mind sleeping on the couch. I'll trade you for the bed if you want."

"No, no, Katie. The couch is more comfortable than my bed back home. Besides, I'm used to sleeping on a couch since I end up falling asleep on it most nights anyway. You know, keeping up with my cases."

"How are all of those going?" I have no idea what to ask, but I know she is interested in them, so I engage with her about it, as she hadn't had much opportunity this week to talk about them.

"Not good. Kyle Hamburg just went to jail."

I remember his name being splashed across every news channel and paper for the last several months. "Why is that *not good*? He did it." I had no idea about this case as I stay away from the news in general.

"That's what I thought, too, until. . . until I *didn't.* They are hiding something. He's just the fall guy."

"Sounds like you have your work cut out for you, then."

She agrees and goes on for nearly an hour about her theories while brushing Dolly's soft curls, prompting her to make the cutest little yawns. I am lulling into sleep, too, until we get a knock at the door.

My mother immediately *shushes me* and mouths, "Who could that be?"

I look at the clock: 7:32 pm. "You act like it's past midnight," I laugh while looking out the peephole. It is Eli and Carter. I swing open the door as fast as possible. "Hi!" I smile and lean in for a hug.

Dolly starts wiggling in my mother's lap as Eli walks in, setting Carter on the floor. Eli embraces me again with one arm. "I hope I'm not interrupting any wedding planning or top-secret girl talk," glancing over at my mother.

She shakes her head, smiling. "Of course not, Eli. I'm so glad to be seeing you again. Katie was just about to make some snacks; do you want anything?"

"I was? I mean," I catch on to my mother's prompt, "yes, I was."

"Sure, then. I'll have what you're having." He gives my forehead a kiss, and I feel my legs melt as I walk to the kitchen.

I am still on the verge of popping from our early dinner feast but decide there is always a little more room for popcorn. I take out a few bags, some chocolate candies, and a few syrups. "Dessert popcorn is coming right up!"

Eli laughs, "I didn't know there was such a thing, and I've never been more excited to try it!"

My mother goes on to tell him about our family's long love of popcorn and its coinciding dental costs each year. "And after a few weeks, I thought I'd be better off just pulling the tooth, when I found out there was a lodged piece of popcorn that had worked its way into my gums. Once they were able to surgically remove it, I felt instant relief."

"Wow. After that, it's brave of you to still eat the stuff."

"What are the chances of getting struck by lightning twice?" she asks rhetorically.

"It might be small, but it's never zero," I add, too busy daydreaming about the hunk on the couch next to my mother to absorb whatever they are talking about.

After everyone polishes off their own bowl, and we run out of bags after making more, Eli and my mother put their feet up on the coffee table while analyzing the websites for Alaska and looking things up online. I stretch out on the floor with the dogs.

"I just tagged you in something funny on my social media, Katie." Eli winks at me, and I feel my cheeks redden quickly.

"Okay, I'll go look right now."

We lovingly gaze into each other's eyes from across the room for a moment.

His phone buzzes in his hand. "I see your mothers already liked it," he turns to her, teasing.

"I get notifications when you post, Eli." She smiles, proud to make the announcement.

I find the post and laugh, holding it up as if I am the first to see it. It is a meme about a dog in a turtleneck, looking like it has good credit.

"Eli, have you looked the hotel up on the internet maps? It's just a few skips away from *sledding!*"

"Of course. I have it right here." He holds up his phone and the two masterminds nod in approval at each other.

"Like dog sledding?" I ask. Both dogs look up at me, and I start laughing at the idea of these two doing any sort of mushing.

"It doesn't say the type. But possibly. Would you enjoy that, Katie?" Eli asks with a smile.

"I've never done any kind of sledding, so I don't know for sure. Don't we need special clothes for that?" I picture Career Day back in school when someone came dressed as a future Iditarod contestant; they came in wearing a head-to-toe suede and fur outfit. Immediately distracted, I decide to search their name on the internet to see if they indeed made it to the Iditarod. Sadly, they did not but instead became a fortune cookie writer. Considering my last one failed to remit the winning lottery numbers, I nearly sent him a message when Eli interrupted my thoughts.

"So, I have a little surprise regarding the clothing part." Eli smiles and my mother replies.

"Oh? And what's that?"

I perk my head up, very eager to hear what that could be.

"My sister offered to take you shopping for our honeymoon. With her generous discount, gift card rewards, and the winter sale happening right now at Norlands, she said she'd fill your entire suitcase as her present to us."

My jaw drops. "Wow! Really? That would be amazing! I'm... speechless!" My mom and I both cheer in excitement.

"Oh, Katie, that sounds like so much fun! I can't wait to help."

Eli and I both laugh and nod our heads.

"I was also wondering how you were feeling about skiing on our honeymoon?"

Eli is quite adventurous, which reminds me that God has a profound sense of humor, considering I am a self-proclaimed homebody. My mother looks over at me above her tablet with a smirk, knowing full well just how uncoordinated I am.

"Oh, skiing? I... I'm not sure, but I think it sounds fun. I've never done it before. Is it hard?"

My mother snorts with laughter and then bows out to go to the kitchen and get something to drink.

"Not if you have a good teacher." Eli flashes his perfect smile.

I can't wait to marry him. "Okay then. Why not?" There are plenty of reasons why I should NOT ski, such as my extreme lack of coordination, but when Eli suggested we go to an adventurous ski resort for our honeymoon, it sounded like a romantic dream and at that moment, I excitedly agree.

"That's my girl."

Eli blows me an air kiss from the couch, and I feel my face redden. My mother is taking her time in the kitchen, thankfully, so we have a few more minutes to discuss it.

"My dad used to take my brother and me when we were kids. I cherish the memories. Of course, it can be challenging to start any sport as an adult because we have different emotions and fears now, but I bet you'll be great at it if you enjoy it. And if not, there is always a wonderful selection of hot chocolate in the lodge with a grand fireplace."

"Since it's important to you, I sincerely would like to try it." And as much as I meant that sentiment, I was imagining a frightening scene from one of those 1980 ski movies in my head. There I would be, on top of K2, donned head to toe in neon windbreaker material on two giant popsicle sticks stuck to my feet with no idea how to get down. I didn't want Eli to know just how disturbed I felt by the idea since I'd already agreed, but then I remembered how good it feels to get out of my comfort zone. Just not right away—hours later, in the lodge like he said, where the hot chocolate was. That would feel great!

There I am, at the peak of the notorious Avalanche Alley, the most extreme double black diamond run at the resort. The weather has been tumultuous, and I've gotten here by mistakenly taking the wrong chairlift—instead of Baby Blue, I took Razors Edge, because I couldn't see which was which. But this is no time for second guessing, because I have to figure out which direction to point the skis to get off this cliff. I overhear someone say "tips down" as they high five another, so I take that as a clue and point my skis towards where I want to go and mumble a prayer.

Judging by the speed of wind hitting my face, I estimate I am going forty miles per hour, and I am quite pleased that I haven't fallen. In fact, I am skiing so smoothly, it feels like I'm not turning or hitting any bumps. I open my eyes as the wind dies down, feeling as though I am slowing, when I realize it is just a squall, and I am still standing in the same place.

I look around as a line forms behind me, as there is one kickoff point to this slope.

"You gonna get some air or what?" the man chewing an offensive amount of Double Bubble behind me asks.

"Catch you on the other side," I confidently call out right before I tip my skis downward, immediately stumbling, and roll the entire descent. When I finally reach the bottom, my skis and poles are gone, but thankfully my neon visor and white sunglasses are still attached to my head.

"Nice yard sale." The gum chewer appears beside me once again at the bottom.

"Excuse me?" I lie there, expecting him to hand me a flyer for antiques being sold off someone's lawn.

He points to my slew of ski gear, trailing all the way down. "You wiped out and all of your gear is scattered. That's called a yard sale." I look at the man with his ball of gum, similar to Greg at work, and can't help but notice he hasn't lent a hand to help me up. As I roll over to get my footing, he disappears.

After a while more, Eli announces it is past Carter's bedtime, but really, I know he is an early-to-bed person, like me, which is another thing I am thankful for.

"So nice to see you, Eli. I do hope you can come over again tomorrow. Katie, what time is our 'Hip-Hop Abs' class? Or did you choose the Booty Burning Bonanza one instead?

Eli lets out a hilarious laugh as I try to hide my embarrassment, but it is too late; there is no going back from this. He puts his arms around me and kisses the top of my head.

"Don't worry, Katie. I think it's cute."

I start laughing, too, and it feels good to be silly.

"Call me when you ladies are home tomorrow and ready for us to come back over. We will bring the snacks this time."

"Okay, that sounds fun," I gush. I can't wait to see him again.

"I love you, Katie Fitzgerald." He kisses me on the cheek, still laughing as he goes out the door, carrying Carter down the steps as I watch them leave.

"Bye, Carter! Grandma will see you tomorrow night!" I close the door behind them and turn to my mother, and we both laugh.

"That was fun," I exclaim as soon as the door shuts, still feeling his presence lingering.

"Yes, I sure do approve of that guy, Katie. Excellent job."

I am thankful for my mother's approval, as I would hate it to be the other way around.

"Thank you, and I'm so glad—".

A shrill cry comes from my mother's throat as she cuts me off, mid-sentence. "It's 8:30 pm! Time for my show! Who wants to watch '*Happily Ever Homicide*?

"How are we related?" I question her while laughing at something else she had said earlier in the evening. "I thought you were going to practice my hairstyle tonight?"

"Of course I am, Katie. Here, sit here on the floor, and I'll do it while I watch. I think this is a repeat, anyway."

She is on her last bobby pin placement when my phone buzzes. It is Eli's sister, Audrey, wanting to schedule our girl's day shopping.

Hello future sister! Eli told me I had the green light to take you to Norlands since he wanted to be the one to surprise you (laughing emoji) (eye roll emoji). I'm off tomorrow, Thursday and Friday of this week. Do any of those work for you?

Thankfully, I have a very generous boss and over three years of unused paid vacation time, so I am able to take the next five weeks off, which gives me another few weeks once we return from our honeymoon to settle in, which will be needed, since we will be looking for a larger place to live, as we each have identical one-bedroom apartments that are full of our things.

With Samantha needing us later in the week, I figure the sooner the better for Audrey.

How about tomorrow? Is it alright that my mom tags along? She's here now.

Audrey replies immediately.

Yes, and yes! I can't wait to meet her. Does 10 a.m. work?
I'm friends with the morning shift, and they've been holding a few
things I wanted you to see.

Absolutely. I can't wait! I reply.

And I can't. I feel like a queen, and this time, it isn't a plastic
crown from *Pretty, Pretty Princess* on my head, but an actual glitzy
tiara my mother has just tried on me for size.

"It looks a little small. Does it feel small? I always forget
how big your head is, Katie. You may have gotten your father's legs,
but you got my head."

"It feels great. Let me see a mirror?" She hands me a small
handheld compact, but it is smeared with lipstick and smells like
breath mints.

"Sorry, this has been rolling around at the bottom of my
purse. I think I'm done with your hair for now, so why don't you get
up and see what you think?"

I instinctively reach to feel my hair, but she swats my hands
away.

"Don't touch it, you'll ruin it. The veil needs to be handled
like crepe paper; it's very delicate. Plus, your hands might be dirty."

I look down at my hands. My nails are meticulously
manicured and not a spot on them as I shuffle to the full-length
mirror in my bedroom.

The hairstyle is a soft half-updo that has braided accents and a soft, gentle curl. My hair doesn't have a single strand out of place, nor does any of it look like I stuck my finger in an electrical socket. The tiara is a little over the top, but overall, *I look like a bride.*

"What do you think?" My mother hollers from the living room, slowly getting up and coming my way.

"I absolutely love it! It's perfect. Do you think the tiara is too much?"

She comes up behind me and stands in the mirror with me, holding Dolly, who now has a small tiara on her head.

"I don't think so at all. It's your day to be as *much* as you want to be."

I laugh at the tiara on Dolly as my mother then reaches for something on the floor outside the room and comes back to the mirror wearing a tiara too. Even Dolly seems to laugh as I reach for my phone and take a photo of the three of us queens.

*****

The next morning, I awake to terribly loud chatter coming from the living room. Not knowing what my mother is up to at this hour, I throw on my bathrobe, scoop up Dolly, and we go to investigate.

We stumble into the brightly lit living room to my mother making hand gestures for us to be quiet. She is wearing a headset, like you'd see on an infomercial operator on daytime television and is in front of her laptop with two ring lights pointed at her from different angles. How she fit those in her suitcase is the biggest mystery, but then again, she did bring several.

"My next caller says he used to dog walk for the neighbors of Kyle's high school girlfriends' parents. He has an interesting point of view and a lens into the life we haven't seen that I think is worth listening to. Let me know in the comments if you agree."

I look at my mother in disbelief—not that she has some sort of show, but that she is shushing me now as I try to open the screen door for Dolly.

"Hello, Bryan? Thanks for calling. Tell us the facts."

"Hi there, Mystery Maven. Long time listener, first time caller."

I roll my eyes, and step out onto the patio, and breathe in the morning air while Dolly, too, seems to enjoy a moment of peace. There is a small patio furniture set that came with the apartment but is so rarely enjoyed because of our torrential rains, but just in time, this morning has clear skies. The chair is wide and stiff, but thanks to the extra plush layers of my bathrobe that my mother swore I'd need to throw away before I marry, it is fine. I debate bringing my coffee out here to enjoy, but the second the thought crosses my mind, I hear the jackhammering start near the business office.

"Dolly, when on earth are they going to be done with that road construction?" She looks up at me with sleepy eyes. "I hope they are done by the time I get back from my honeymoon." The thought makes every blood cell in my body do the jumping bean dance. I can't wait to become Mrs. Eli Skatey.

I hold Dolly closer, giving her a kiss on her head. "Grandma Mystery Maven is going to watch you and Carter while we are away. I'll make sure to check-in every day, okay?" She nestles her little curls into my neck. In the last few months of our time together, we've grown very attached to one another, and thankfully she feels the same about Eli since he's consistently been here the entire time. She and Carter get along swimmingly and thankfully like different toys, though Dolly has been coming around on the squeakers. She usually goes for the soft and fuzzy, while Carter likes the plastic or bouncy ones.

Eli and I steal away any time we can and take them to the Bark Park, so we can spend time together. We're also regulars at Yappy Hour, the dog bakery, and we've dropped in on a few doggy daycares and boarding facilities for tours, as we may have days where we can't take them with us somewhere.

Since Eli's lease will expire at the end of this month, and our honeymoon will be past the date, he was able to finagle a two-week extension and the day we get home, he will start to move into my apartment while we shop for a new place to live, as then my lease will end a few months later.

The leasing office is a funky bunch of people. One might assume that anyone in that profession might be miffed about a tenant moving out, but when we let them know that we would be leaving to find a larger place, they were so over the moon for Eli and I that they went as far as hosting an engagement party for us in the clubhouse. It was a small affair and only attended by the few people who know us in our complex, including my neighbors, Marge and Patricia and their dogs. Since they don't offer larger apartments, we will look for ones elsewhere once we get back from our honeymoon. The idea of it excites me as much as it horrifies me, and I still pinch myself that this is all happening.

I look back to the day just a few months ago that I was sitting in the Three Maples Church parking lot talking to a woman with tears in her eyes about feeling defeated. I was lonely and she was bursting at the seams with pets who wanted to love someone. Little did I know that the next day, I would be meeting my future husband at the most unlikely place of all: the Bark Park. So now, it's become our tradition as we continue to learn and grow our love on the Pawrent benches.

Finally, it sounds like my mother has wrapped up whatever she is doing, and I slide open the door and step back into my apartment.

"Sorry about that, Katie. There was a break in the case, and I couldn't leave my followers hanging."

"And what was that?" I put Dolly in front of her food bowl while my mother explains.

"I found Bryan online."

"The dog walker?" I pour some Kibbles into Dolly's dish.

"Yes, a lucky break indeed. He says that Kyle's high school girlfriend broke up with him after he gave her one of those ghost peppers, you know the ones—the ones that are so hot, they could *kill*."

Today is looking like I will need more caffeine than usual, so I dump half the bag of coffee into my machine.

"So now, I have a possible psychopath on my hands."

"I thought you said Kyle was innocent. And how is that psychopath-"

She cuts me off. "INNOCENT? I said no such thing. I said he's the fall guy for someone else. But was he involved? Abso-freakin-*lutely*, Katie."

"Alright, it's a little too early for this, isn't it? It's not even seven yet, and Audrey is taking us shopping today. Can you be on your best behavior, please? Also, are you planning on giving roadside assistance, or can you remove the headset?"

"Fine," she laughs as she tears the headset off. "I better call and check on your dad and see if he likes the hotel."

"Wait, what?" I nearly drop my coffee cup.

"They flew in yesterday, him and Edward. There isn't any room here, so I figured he'd get a hotel."

"I thought they weren't coming until the day before the wedding?"

"You know I can't be away from Edward that long. What's your point, Katie?" My mother was only half listening as she pulled out her phone.

"When were you planning on mentioning that my father and... my little 'brother' was in town?" I used air quotes as she insisted that we refer to Edward as my brother to make him *more comfortable in his adjustment,* though he's been *adjusting* for the last seven years and is still an absolute terror.

"We've been busy, Katie. When did I have time?"

"I don't know, last night we were all just laying around eating popcorn, which might have been convenient to slip that into our conversation?"

"I guess I've just been having too much fun here with you to remember. Oh, I really do miss my little Eddie. We should go see him today!"

My mother takes Dolly for a short walk outside to stretch her legs while I shower and get dressed. I know I'll be trying on a lot of clothes today, so I opt for something loose and comfortable with some slip-on shoes. When my mother comes back to the house, she looks at me up and down and smirks.

"What's that look?" I ask, putting my hands on my hips.

"You still have a few more days until you can wear the 'I've given up' ensemble," she emphasizes by using air quotes.

"First of all, this is *in* right now. It's a onesie type overall that everyone is wearing." I look down at the outfit, feeling the description is as hideous as the look.

"It looks like you're wearing an adult diaper."

"Ugh." I hate it, but she is right. "Fine, I'll change," I say, storming off and slipping into some plain leggings, black boots, and a flowy blouse. When I return to the living room, she looks up at me over her reading glasses and nods in approval.

The aroma of food wafts up my nostrils. "That smells delicious—what are you making?"

"An apple cinnamon French toast. It's a new recipe I found online."

"I'm surprised you have any free time online outside of your *Mystery Maven-ness.*"

She looks down at the bread sizzling in the frying pan. "Truthfully, I'm trying to take a step back from it all. It's taken a bit of a turn for the worse, I'm afraid."

"How so?"

"I have somewhat of a crazed fan base," she speaks quietly.

I can't tell if there is fear in her voice or sarcasm.

"It started out so innocently—" she says as she turns off the stovetop and spins around to face me, "—just a video sharing my thoughts regarding a case. That one a few years ago, where the guy, Corky Myers, dressed up as a hotdog, broke into the condiment warehouse, and switched all the machine labels?"

I nodded, remembering the horror as mustard filled ketchup bottles and mayonnaise filled mustard. Since it was all automated, they didn't discover the problem until products started shipping to stores.

"Well after I published that video, *'Just to be frank,'* it went *viral.* The famous fashionista model, Trixie Von Suds, shared it, and from there, it spread like *wildfire.*"

"The heiress to the *Sparkle Dish Soap* fortune?" I shake my head, lost in translation at what exactly the problem was.

"Yes, that's her. You might not assume that someone in that line of work has much of an online presence, but she's quite famous online. She doesn't need to work, but she still rakes in the big bucks, thanks to a bidding war for a partnership with Big Sponge. Anyway, all ninety-nine million of her followers saw it, including the fugitive *wiener* in question." She shudders at the thought.

"Oh my. *Is he after you now?*" I lower my voice, concerned we might be *bugged* before immediately realizing I'm falling into my mother's true crime trap.

"No, nothing like that." She shakes her head, adamantly. "It's much worse. He's saying I helped his case since he was acquitted; but all I pointed out was there were multiple sightings of a man in a hot dog costume that night, and since they couldn't pick him out of a lineup, how do they know which was which?"

"A very rational thought, indeed." I nod back to her.

"Well, now he's found himself in another heap of trouble: He dressed up as a chicken and egged the governor's mansion. He's putting quite a bit of pressure on me to make another video that will help his case, but this one isn't so black and white, I'm afraid."

"Oh no. I had no idea you were going through this! Is he threatening you?"

"No. I suppose in his own way, he thinks I'm his friend. But I never intended to get this deep with someone online. He's now showing up in places I frequent, like the grocery store and frankly," she starts to smile at her own pun, but it quickly fades from her lips, "I'm beginning to be creeped out."

"Could that be a coincidence? Everyone needs groceries." I try to be the rational voice, but I, too, am feeling a little disturbed. She starts to plate our food, pulling out the maple syrup from the fridge.

"At first, I thought so. But then I was at the eye doctor getting an exam when I saw out of the corner of my eye someone in a *Kool-Aid man* costume walk by the open door. A week later, I was browsing the discount bin of makeup at the drug store because I know how much you like makeup shades that no one else does, and I looked up to see a giant corn cob in the opposite aisle from me. But the scariest incident?" She opens the bottle of syrup and starts generously pouring over a plate of French toast. "You know those inflatable waving characters that car dealerships put on their corners because they think that attracts customers in some weird way?"

"Yes."

"I woke up one morning with one in my yard. Square in the center, lit up and everything, plugged into a small generator. For some reason, that *terrified me.*"

A shiver goes down my spine; not to her story, but that she is still pouring syrup. "Is that your plate?" I ask as the syrup is starting to pool and spill.

"No, it's yours. Here you go." She places it on the small kitchen island where I have two barstools. On the other plate, she just puts a tablespoon of syrup and seats herself with it.

"So, what are you going to do?" I ask as I try to get a bite of French toast that won't send me into diabetic shock.

"I hate to ask, Katie. But would you mind if I talked to your boss about it? I'm considering a restraining order."

"Of course I don't mind. I'll call him right now if you want?" I pull out my phone and scan the contacts for my aptly named boss, Frank, but she interjects.

"No—it can wait. Let's go enjoy our day. There aren't any mascots or giant food products following me onto the plane. I'm safe out here; I can do it after the wedding while I'm pet sitting."

I smile at the thought of her staying to watch the dogs. Dolly, on cue, comes waltzing up with a toy in her mouth.

"Come here, sweetie. Grandma is talking about you." I pick up her small, fuzzy body and let her sniff my plate. She isn't interested. "Do you want any more coffee?" I ask my mother, whose cup is nearly empty.

"Yes, but just a little more. I want the shakes, not tremors."

Chapter 4
Tales From The Leash
Carolyn

I never thought I'd be happy about getting a wedding invitation in the mail from my ex-fiancé but today proved different.

Maybe it was because of my relationship with Micah, who could literally be on the cover of those good-looking firefighter calendars that raise money for puppies or something, or because I really changed since I've committed my life to Christ.

Six months ago, I hit rock bottom in my life. Nothing was going right... I hated my job, hated my environment... I hated my life. I've been ready for marriage longer than I can remember and yet, every man I ever met fell short of my expectations, starting with dumping the man I was looking at on this wedding invitation, Eli Skatey. I battled with regret because of this, and yet, I did it again and again. Every time a man expressed more than an initial interest in me, I scoured him for faults until I found them.

With Eli, it was both the easiest and hardest decision I've ever made. On one end, I will not marry a man who isn't committed to living for the Lord. On the other hand, had I waited, would he have become the man he is today? Or was our breakup a necessary event that altered both of our lives for good?

Now that I've met Micah, I no longer wish I would have waited it out. There was a time, very recently in fact, that I wished Eli would have considered giving us another shot. . . yes. I thought we could pick up where we left off, literally, with an engagement. But I see now that he was right. It was too late for us. And his meeting his future wife, Katie, who first met Micah, well... It's hilarious how interwoven that situation was, and once again proves just how much God has a sense of humor. It made me admire Katie so much, and I know that Eli is in good hands with her. Not that he needs my approval, or that I'd ever tell him that. But Katie turned down Micah, who's a drop dead good-looking, animal-loving firefighter who saves kittens from trees and puppies from burning buildings. How much more perfect does someone get? And I thank Katie for planting the seed in his mind about God. He soon after committed his life to Christ, and then we met. If they hadn't met at the dog park that day, and that meant Katie hadn't shared the message with him, would I have been able to do it? I don't think so. Knowing me, I would've dropped him like a hot potato.

With Micah, there are flaws. But this time around, I am embracing them. For instance, he's into movies. Okay, that's not anything harmful, and we go see every single new movie that comes out, even if it doesn't interest either of us, right? Well, you know when you're in a movie theater and hear someone laughing without abandon at any old crack? The slightest joke, funny or not, there's always that one person, right? It's Micah. He's the equivalent of a "clapper" on infomercials. At first, I was completely shocked and upset. I could've broken up with him, but I was ready to turn a new leaf, so I prayed over it. "Lord, this guy is so great, but I'm so embarrassed to be around him like this."

Then it was the quoting of said flicks. At first, I assumed he was just the type to discuss a movie, which was fun, because I've never dated anyone who's shown so much interest in what I think. So, we give each other our personal reviews, what we liked and didn't like about the movie, and so on. But then a few days go by, and he said something that I don't understand.

"Be a good boy, Jimbo!" he hollered as he walked me to my car after a brutal workout at the gym together.

"Umm... What now?" I stared at him, completely confused, and he laughed.

"You know, from *The Great Jimboni* movie we saw last week. About the guy who rode the Zamboni down the wedding aisle?"

I stared at him blankly, nodding. "How could I forget?"

He kissed his perfect lips to mine and said goodnight as I got into my car, with him shutting it behind me. I watched his rippling, muscular physique get into his truck as I started my vehicle and drove away, trying to figure out what just happened. Am I in a relationship with a dork that quotes movies? And am I utterly in love with him? It was yes to both.

God showed me the freedom in removing judgment from others. When I stopped looking at Micah through a critical lens that no one would ever be able to live up to, I found myself head over heels in love. Micah represented unabashed joy. He took life at face value and never felt afraid to take part in something. While I feel self-conscious trying something new, if I take Micah, he'll be the life of the party before it is over. And that's one of the many reasons why I fell in love with him and his spirit. He's not just a beautiful man to look at, but he's become my perfect man on the inside, too. The things I felt were imperfections, now I find to be hilarious. I've embraced his movie junkie ways and started collecting the perfect candies and popcorns to stock my pantry with for our movie marathons.

I am a far from perfect person who's been all but consumed with her *image* to the point that I had little substance inside. Micah is not my first go around with a serious relationship, but this is the first time that I feel accepting of who they are and what love they bring. God gave me a perfectly imperfect partner, Micah, as my daily reminder that I will not judge someone for their joy. I will not judge someone for their choices in life. Their hobbies and interests. Their past. These are all the things that make us unique, and God created us in His image. Micah is forgiven, just as I am, and now we are two people washed clean in the Holy Spirit, starting new.

Now, if Micah wants to include a movie quote in his wedding vows, that might be a different story. He hasn't popped the question yet, but we both know this is it. We want to spend the rest of our lives together as soon as we can. Next weekend, he is taking me to Wyoming to meet his parents. They live on a cowboy ranch, where Micah grew up. He is going to take me horseback riding, and I can't wait to see him in a cowboy hat.

He is close with his family, and I have a sneaking suspicion that this is the final step in our relationship before he will ask me to marry him.

Chapter 5
Paw & Order
Katie

It is about time to leave for our shopping day with Eli's sister Audrey, and we decide that Dolly will come with us, as we aren't sure how long today will take.

"Get her dressed while I run to the car, will you?" I laugh but know she is serious, and I pull out a simple sweater for her to wear over her harness. But before I put it on, I remember this is a special time to spend with family, and so I pull out the sparkle ball gown with matching collar and dress Dolly to the nines. Grabbing my pink rain slicker, I carry her downstairs as my mother loads Dolly's car seat into her rental and puts her stroller attachment in the hatchback, turning to me.

"Well, look who's finally come around?" She joyously picks up Dolly and holds her in her arms, dancing her around like they are at a ball in a beast's castle.

A wave of dizziness hits me once again, and this time my mother catches me before I fall.

"Katie! What's happening? Do we need to go to the emergency room?"

Her voice of true concern upsets me, because up until now, I was thinking this had passed. "I- I don't think so. I'm fine. It's passed." I am hit with an extreme plunge of nausea that I can't hold in as I kneel next to my car and release the contents of my stomach.

"What in the world-—that's it, Katie. We are going to the doctor. I'll call Audrey and tell her we are running late."

The instantaneous relief I felt after throwing up was palpable as I waved my mother off the phone. "Really, I think that was it. I feel amazing now. Let me just go freshen up, and I'll be right back." I silence her protests with my brisk walk up the stairs to my apartment and wash my face and brush my teeth. As I walk past my kitchen on the way back to the car, I consider the syrupy breakfast and wonder if that had upset my internal apple cart that much. Considering I barely had any at all, and I genuinely hadn't felt hungry yet today, I know that isn't it. I lock up my apartment and make a decision.

"Okay, I feel fine now, truly. Don't worry about it. But I am going to make a doctor's appointment, just in case. I don't want some weird gut issue haunting me on my honeymoon."

"I think that's wise, Katie. Try Dr. Brand, over at the Newtown Clinic. She has incredible reviews and a real knack for internal medicine." I laugh as I pull out my phone and type in the name. At this point, I accept the fact that my mother knows absolutely everything and just go with it.

"Good morning, Katie." Marge calls over to me, seeing I have company.

"Hi, Marge! This is my mother—".

She cuts me off. "Oh, I know her! We've been friends online since you moved in."

My mother walks over to Marge, still holding Dolly, and gives her a one-arm hug. "So nice to see you, Marge."

I still can't quite wrap my head around this, as my mother has never been out here before. "Um, what now?"

"C'mon, Katie, we better not be late for Audrey."

Marge calls back, "Have fun at Norlands!"

"How did you—".

"Thanks, Marge! Text you later," my mother shouts out as she gets behind the wheel. She never ceases to surprise me.

The second we pull out of my parking spot, I dial the clinic number and speak to the scheduler. After explaining my symptoms and concerns with my upcoming wedding and honeymoon being so near, she puts me on hold and returns a moment later with a resolution.

"Sometimes Dr. Brand takes extra appointments after hours, and considering what you have going on, she has agreed to see you tomorrow at 5 p.m., if that works?"

I feel relieved. "Yes, that would be incredible. Thank you so much." I give her the required insurance information, reading off from the little card I've carried around since I started working at the law firm, but hardly use outside of the scheduled checkups.

We pull up to Norlands just as I get off the phone, and I tell my mother about tomorrow's appointment.

"That sounds like Dr. Brand; always going the extra mile."

"Can we not tell Eli about this? Until we know what it is, I mean. No need to get him involved if it's something minor," I plead with her, knowing that she is an iron vault of secrecy, but she also loves Eli like family. And family is where secrets slip.

"Are you sure, Katie? He's your future husband. You've got to clue him in on these things if you're going to do life together. Even if it's something embarrassing, like that illness I contracted on the cruise that you like to remind me of. There's nothing off limits."

I put my finger up to interrupt her. "While I understand the sentiment, there's got to be *some* boundaries. You know, to keep things romantic and all."

We both laugh together, and it feels good, and I decide I will tell Eli... the next time I see him. For now, I will let him get through his workday while I enjoy my time with Audrey. I send him a text to let him know I am here.

Just got to Norlands. I'm so excited! (heart emoji) (bride emoji) (mountain emoji) (heart emoji)

(Typing...)

Not as excited as I am to be your husband.

My heart feels like it skips seventeen beats as I read his message, feeling the warmth in my cheeks spread to my forehead and neck.

"KATIE! ARE YOU HAVING A STROKE?" my mother shouts in the parking lot at me as I stare back at her quizzically.

"No?"

"Why are you beet red?" She puts a hand on her hip.

"Are beets red? I've seen golden ones."

"You have sweat on your upper lip."

If she is convinced I am having a medical emergency, she has a weird way of showing it.

"It's just warm in this coat, is all."

Leaning in, she whispers, *"You better get that waxed before the big day."*

She gives me a wink before spinning around on her heels and pushing Dolly's stroller into the front doors. I run a finger over my upper lip and nod in agreement.

Audrey is all over Dolly when we walk inside. Her excitement for shopping is contagious, and soon, we are all speaking very animatedly. Dolly is an absolute angel for Audrey, and I am so pleased when she gives her cheek a little lick.

"I just love getting *puppy kisses* from a *purr-fect wittle angel bubby*, don't I *sweetie pie honey bunches?*" Audrey insists we start to browse the racks she pulled while she and Dolly catch up; they roll around on the floor for quite some time before Dolly is lovingly placed back into her stroller. "Okay, now that that's out of the way..."

Audrey and my mother start chuckling to themselves and speak about how sweet it is that Dolly and Carter have found each other again, separated at birth to be reunited as siblings later.

"It's such a unique love story, Katie, and Eli. It really shows the way God works is more than just mysterious—it's glorious! To unite these two with their matching dogs—that may or may not be related—I couldn't have dreamed it up if I wanted to."

I smile as my mother beams with pride, pulling out her camcorder from her purse, and then my smile goes away.

"Katie is here with her future sister-in-law, Audrey, as they shop for Katie and Eli's Alaskan honeymoon!"

I nervously look at my mother, reminding her with my eyes that she has promised to be on her best behavior. Audrey doesn't miss a beat and jumps in front of the camera. "I have lots of things already picked out; shall we show you now?"

"Yes, let's see them!" my mother exclaims, clearly loving how Audrey takes the lead.

The first item she pulls from the other end of the rack is a beautiful, simple, black sweater dress that has a little flare to the love sleeves along with a boat neckline. "This will be perfect for a night at the lodge. You'll be sipping hot cocoa, planning your future, and gazing into each other's eyes lovingly."

I close my eyes and daydream, *loving every second* of Audrey's description.

"Albeit it's very slimming, too. I might need one of those in my size, Audrey." my mother chimes in, smiling from behind the camera. "Don't worry, Katie. I won't wear it if you and I might be seen in the same vicinity."

I shoot her a look usually reserved for inmates in padded cells, and she nods, putting the camera back into her suspiciously large purse. *I should've known she had it;* why else would she be carrying around a purse the size of a diaper bag?

The next item is a smart pair of waterproof pants and a matching black jacket. "These are lined with a moisture wicking fleece material. Best to be worn over some long johns— they're perfect for a romantic snowshoe around the property, and the belt on the coat makes it very *figure flattering,"* she winks.

Eli had mentioned she won awards for personal shopping and now I know why; she is *brilliant.*

"This also doubles as your skiing outfit, Katie. Eli told me the good news that you two will be reliving one of his favorite memories with our brother."

This was the first time I've heard Audrey speak of her brother who passed, so I'm not sure how to handle it. "I hope it's as meaningful as he remembers... And that I can stay upright!"

Audrey and my mother roar; both happily agreeing that the chances of that are slim for someone's first day on skis. I start to notice the chemistry Audrey and my mother share, and I feel joyous that my family gets along so well.

Just the thought of my family growing, as I am marrying into another set of parents, a sister-in-law that's wonderful, and the husband of my dreams makes my mind float for several minutes while they get on about some hilarious story when Audrey took her fiancé skiing for the first time.

"It was the first time I saw him panic, and he was nearly in tears. I also found out he is deathly afraid of heights, which is fine by me. I have no desire to be in there longer than I must, either!"

There have been many things I've been eager to try for the attention of a guy I thought I liked, such as going to a horseback riding ranch with a middle school interest, Lee. His parents were equestrians and horse trainers, and while we were only thirteen years old, I remember how expected it was that everyone had not only ridden a horse, but mastered the art. When he left his birthday party invitation at my desk before I sat down, not knowing that Claire and I had switched desks that day, I was so honored to attend, that I begged my mother to buy me fringe chaps to wear over my Levi's. Claire was disappointed, as she was friends with his sister, and I had never so much as spoken to him, but that's showbiz, baby.

The following weekend at Lee's party, I was a fish out of water in my cowboy getup. It doesn't matter that the only accessories we could find were from the party store; I felt like the Lone Ranger until I realized it wasn't that kind of party. People wore little helmets that looked like half the shell of a walnut and made their heads look bulbous. Instead of cowboy boots, they wore tall, knee-high pirate boots and skintight clothing that outlined their butts in a way that made me uncomfortable. These weren't cowboys at all. But I wasn't going to go out like this, in shame.

Before I arrived, my biggest fear was that someone would be wearing the same outfit as me, and we'd have to pretend we'd done it on purpose. Little did I know I would unlock new nightmares for the rest of my life after Lee's parents put me on a horse that hated the sound of my voice, and every time I spoke, it would try and buck me off. "Help, please." The horse, whose name was Mr. Boo, kept jumping around on his front legs as if he was going to stand up on his hindquarters.

"Mr. Boo, what is wrong?" Lee's mother questioned the horse like it was going to communicate back to her. "That's so unusual for him; he's a child's pony, for crying out loud. Gary, can you come over here? I've never seen him display this behavior before."

"Can someone help me down?" The moment I spoke, he started clawing at the ground with his hooves in an unpredictable manner and had wrangler Gary not plucked me from the saddle one second later, this would be another kind of story. "Umm... What was that?" I asked as Lee's mom walked me back to where the other kids had been waiting for their turn.

The woman shook her head, her walnut helmet not moving an inch, unlike my hat that needed the strings tightened. "That was unusual, I'm sorry. I think it might be the clothes you're wearing. I don't think he's ever seen so many sequins, which is hard to top, because he used to walk in the Mardi Gras parades."

"Katie, are you quietly reliving the time you called your kindergarten teacher 'mom,' or are you with us?" My mother snaps me back to reality as Audrey steps into the back room to grab the next round of items to show us.

I ramble off, "horse, birthday party" and my mother knows exactly what I am talking about.

"I saw Lee's mom years later at the grocery store, and she told me that Mr. Boo had nothing but problems after that day. That is until they dressed him up like a showgirl. Turns out he was just insanely jealous of your shiny outfit. In all my years of solving cases, I truly did not see that coming."

I am fully engaged until I notice Audrey walking back out with some very *delicate* looking items.

"Alright... I have another few items now that the camera is put away." She laughs, and I suddenly feel nervous, letting out a breath when she holds up a bathing suit. "I saw in the brochure Eli gave me, there's an outdoor jacuzzi tub!" The swimsuit is a beautiful emerald green with a matching coverup skirt and a darling topknot headband. "This tone really brings out your eyes, and the headband will help that hair of yours."

We all laugh. Over the next half hour, she pulls out striped silk pajamas with matching slippers, faux-fur mukluk boots, scarves, heavy mittens, and a purse backpack. I am so blown away by her generosity that I start to tear up.

"Audrey, I don't even have the words to thank you. Just. . . wow. I appreciate this more than you know." It isn't just the gifts, but the styling; left to my own devices I would be sporting muumuus and coveralls on my honeymoon.

"You are so welcome, Katie. You deserve it, and I want you to have a beautiful life with my brother. I have one more thing I want you to try on." She smiles, revealing her beaming, radiant teeth.

I must know who her dentist is. Audrey reaches for a shoe box that is hidden behind the rack. She opens it up, revealing the most beautiful high heel boots I've ever seen. They look quilted, like a designer handbag, and have a beautiful, rich gold zippered up back. When I slip my foot inside, it is met with a cushiony pillow base along with an arch support I cannot, from this moment on, live without.

"Oh MY! Can I never take these off?" I laugh but mean it. They are a dream, and the tears start flowing *for real.* Audrey hugs me, and then my mom, who is now also crying in joy, picks up Dolly.

"Thank you," I choke out, and she nods and smiles.

"I'm so glad you like everything."

"I don't like it; I LOVE IT!"

She laughs and says she will be right back, as she takes a piece of paper to the register with the items' barcodes already printed out. They ring her up and add in her discount and coupons, plus her manager had worked out another small discount on top of it all. She pays and comes back to say she is pleased with the outcome.

"I'll have all of this wrapped up, and it will be ready for pickup later, if that works? I want to properly pack it into your suitcase for you." She takes a step closer to us, lowering her voice. "Along with that nightgown I saw you eyeing."

She points to a pink gown that looks like something a 1950's starlet would wear to a movie premier; I had admired it, because I couldn't believe something so beautiful would be reserved for sleeping. Audrey and my mother erupt with laughter as my cheeks return to shades of berry.

"Katie, it looks like you're wearing those roadkill-colored blushers you used to like as a kid."

"Gee, thanks!" I laugh, fanning my face with my hands.

My mother loves to remind me of the fact that I used to wear any makeup I could find in the clearance section of the drugstore. Back in the day where anything they were trying to get rid of would be put into a plastic bin on the ground, and you'd have to practically get on all fours to sort through-—that was the stuff I picked out, and I had the nickname 'Grape Face' at school to go with it.

An unfortunate nickname, but I was going through some sort of phase, dabbling in makeup shades that made my face look like tomato sauce-stained Tupperware with the dreaded makeup line ending in various places around my jawline. It was a year into this look that one of my mom's friends, Selma, grabbed my face, looked me dead in the eye and gave me the wisdom I'll never forget: "No amount of blending is going to fix this, kid." Timeless advice that could be applied to many aspects of my life forever.

The dark makeup had stained all my shirt collars, pillows, and towels for good. It was the kind of makeup that would transfer onto any surface—it went on like a shellac and never quite dried, giving that 'I'm severely sweaty' vibe all day. Thankfully, after my mom's friend guided me to the shades more apt to match my skin color with names like Porcelain and Alabaster, I turned into a white sheet that was soon to discover a makeup product I'd never be able to get enough of for the next ten years: blush. But immediately after this intervention, I was only buying ones with names like Black Rose and Merlot, sourced from those discount bins at the dime store. "Mom, can I get this? It's only ten cents!"

"Sure," my mother would reply, not looking at the blush that was surely created as a watercolor for dead roses and mistakenly put into a pan and sold for makeup.

"Shall we go get some lunch, girls?" Audrey asks, recommending a place to take Dolly outside beforehand.

"I just happen to be starved," I smile at my mother who mutters something about cooking for me this morning but also laughing.

"We could try one of those dog-friendly cafes Katie's always going on about?" My mother asks Audrey as if I don't have a say, but that sounds perfect to me as I pick up Dolly from her stroller and give her a kiss on her head.

"I'd love that! Give me say, twenty minutes to wrap things up here, to finish gathering it up, and I'll be on my way!"

We leave Norlands, emotionally exhausted from all the unexpected love I'd received.

"That was so much fun!" My mother calls out as we get into the car. "I just love his family. Especially his mom!"

I turned to her, about to ask when and where they had met when my phone chimes with a text message. It is Eli.

How was my bride's shopping trip? I melt into my seat.

It was so much fun! I can't believe how much your sister got for me. Feeling very blessed! I can't wait to wear everything on our honeymoon!
(Typing...)
(Typing...)
I can't wait to see you model your new wardrobe on our trip. (heart emoji)

My heart leaps with joy as I picture us having a romantic dinner in the lodge, followed by the outdoor tub. Suddenly, I remember *just how pale* I had looked in the bathing suit. Surely that would be the norm for Alaskans in the winter, though, so I may get lucky and blend right in.

"Should I get a spray tan?"

My mother nearly slams the breaks when I ask. "I thought you'd never ask! I'll schedule a spray for both of us at *Basking Buns* in a few days."

"You've only been here a few days, and you already know the businesses?" I look at her in amazement.

"Katie, for a paralegal, I'm a little disappointed in your lack of research on your town's offerings."

We both giggle and start to talk about spray tan prep so we won't turn orange and laugh that my mother should go first in case it is.

We meet with Audrey and have a wonderful lunch during the weekday Yappy Hour. Audrey shares about her own fiancé and about the wedding they have been planning for seven months.

"We should have just eloped." She puts her head in her hands, rocking back and forth. "He's got a mother in the form of my worst nightmare."

"Oh no! Please, go on." My mother motions to the waiter to bring another Whippet Sour Mocktail.

"Well, I told her I didn't want a bridal shower, right? Because we were doing a huge rehearsal dinner, plus the wedding, so it was just one less thing people needed to attend, one less day to take off work, and most importantly, one less gift I just don't need."

"Completely reasonable," I said while slicing through my wedge salad.

"Yeah—she didn't think so. And you know what she did? She planned her own shower to accept the praise and gifts for her future grandchildren, while she ignores the child I already have. She calls it a *Grandma Shower.*"

"That's just corrupt." My mother shook her head in disbelief. "Have you ever pulled a file on her?"

"What do you mean?" Audrey sips her Barkberry Soda, shaking her head in confusion.

"Oh, you know, *get a background check on Mother Dearest.*"

I put my head in my hands.

"No, I didn't even consider that. I guess I'd rather not. I mean... I couldn't explain that to Jeff if he found out..."

"What if, say, I did it for you?" My mother grins ear to ear, already pulling up her account on *imwatchingyou.org*, turning her phone around to show Audrey. "All I need is Mrs. Dahmer's first name."

"Mother?" I croak out and my voice reaches the highest octave. Thankfully, she snaps out of it but gently pulls her phone away in case Audrey decides to take her up on it. I glance at Audrey, who has a look of fear in her eyes before she breaks out in hysterical laughter.

"You two just *kill me!* If I didn't know any better, I'd think you were serious. Adding in the Dahmer name?" She nearly chokes, "I don't think I've laughed this hard in years!"

I release all the breath in my lungs I've been holding for the last minute and return to my salad. Audrey goes back to sharing the other horrifying facts about her soon-to-be in-laws.

"And that's just the beginning of it unfortunately. Our honeymoon will be at the Pink Palms Hotel in Hawaii, right?"

I close my eyes thinking of all the fun trips I had to look forward to with Eli.

"Thankfully, my parents are taking my son, Connor, for the week but now, I wish she had offered because of what she's done. She just happened to book her birthday trip at the same hotel, for the same week we are there."

"NO!" My mother slams her fist down at the table, causing a few dogs to bark throughout the cafe. Audrey just nods and looks like she is going to start crying.

"You know Audrey, I just read the most interesting article about the psychological mind of a mother-in-law. Apparently, things can change when your child meets their spouse. How about I send it to you so you can get a little more insight into the criminal mind?"

"That would be great, I'll give you my email."

"No need, I have it." My mother goes back to her Asian stir fry.

So many questions, but I choose where to start, "Criminal mind?"

"What's that, Katie?"

Audrey sighs. "It's not like... It's not like I haven't done this before, so in a sense, I know how things can be. Jeff is my true match, but if Kyle hadn't left me for the mailwoman, I would've still been happy with him. We had an easy relationship, but probably because he was an orphan."

My mother nods. "It's the three M's. You can't turn a blind eye to the mailman, milkman, or the mother-in-law." She shakes her head. I don't have anything to add, so I take a big bite of my salad.

"I just don't know how to tell my fiancé that more than anything, I want to marry him barefoot on a beach, in a dress off the rack, and skip all the rest. If it wasn't for the pressures of this wedding being his mother's event of the century, we would've been married a year ago. We just want to start our lives together, but neither one of us has brought it up."

"Tell him just that. I think that's beautiful." I put my hand on hers and she agrees.

"You know what? You're right. I will. He's taking me to dinner tonight, and it's time I share my feelings."

"Keep me posted how that goes, will you?" I smile at her.

"I will, but I'm going to need lots of prayers from my ladies." Audrey has my hand in her left, and she takes my mother's hand in her right. "Dolly, that means you too!" Dolly looks up from her small dish of crunchy vegetables and some sort of pate.

"I'll be sure she has her paws crossed for you tonight." My mother smiles.

"How old is Connor?" my mother asked while she twirled a piece of her stir fry onto a fork.

Audrey beams. "He just turned eleven. I love that kid with my whole heart! He's quite a whiz at math, it turns out. I don't know where he got it from, since we all know his father can't even add up his child support, and he certainly didn't get it from me!" Audrey laughs. "But really, though, he's a great kid. His dad walking out was so hard on us, but that kid ended up being more of a champ about it than I was. And then when we met Jeff at church, Connor was the one that suggested we have him over for pizza. Invited him over right then and there, on the spot. My jaw dropped! What a matchmaker, am I right?"

"It sounds like you've been through some mud, Audrey. But you've found your way, and you're now marrying what sounds like a wonderful man. I'm so happy to have you as a part of our family, too." My mother reaches over and gives Audrey a hug.

We stop by Norlands on our way back to my apartment to pick up the clothing that was so generously purchased for me. Audrey had instructed me it would be ready for pickup at the customer service counter, to which when I arrive, they wheel out a gorgeous shiny navy suitcase that spins around effortlessly. It is full of stunning clothes and complete with an embroidered luggage tag that reads '*Mrs.* 'It is the most beautiful suitcase I've ever seen. I am overwhelmed by Aubrey's generosity and will arrange a 'thank you' floral bouquet to her home.

"Congratulations on your wedding," the woman tells me as I gently roll the suitcase out the front doors.

"Thank you," I beam back.

The rest of the day is spent doing errands and planning. We drop Dolly off at the apartment for a nap while we go to visit my father and Edward at the hotel. They are both lounging and watching television just like they are still at home. I am surprised just how comfortable the two of them are together now, after getting off on such a rough start. "So, you two are just the best of buds now?" I look at them as my father is sitting up on the bed and Edward is next to him.

"It took a while, but we came to an understanding. If your mother isn't in the room, he is accepting of me. But the moment he makes eye contact with her, something goes wrong in his mind and his instinct is to kill me. I don't know why that is, but let me just say, there's only so many emergency room visits you can take before they start to ask questions."

"Oh, don't listen to him, Katie. One social worker shows up to investigate our home life and your dad freaks out."

My jaw drops. "A social worker came... to your home?" I can't believe this is the first time I have heard about this.

"Yes, Louise came and agreed that your father and Edward needed some real bonding time. Hopefully on this trip, they will fall in love with each other, and Edward won't feel like such an outsider."

I shoot a glance at my father, who is shaking his head as he puts on wrist wraps. "What are those for?"

He smiles and lifts his eyebrows, looking at me with tight eyes. "Watch this."

He retrieves a small dog treat from his pocket and holds it out to Edward, but while his arm gets increasingly closer to the little dog, a deep guttural growl starts forming in him. "Here, Edward. It's a treat. I'm your friend, remember?" My father tries to coax the little dog to eat the biscuit, and I watch as the little hairs on the back of his small body begin to stand up, while the growling gets louder. Edward reveals his teeth, and his eyes go wild, lashing out at my father and grabbing him by the wrist. I'm not sure if he draws blood, but my father lets out a small cry.

"Are you going to do something?" I turn to my mother as she watches.

"This is between them, Katie." She looks at her watch. "We better get going. I want to stop by the post office and see if my copy of *The Wedding Veil Killer* has arrived."

We say goodbye to my father and Edward and make a few plans for when we'll all get together again.

"So, pizza tomorrow with Eli, and in two days, we are going to get together with his parents. Can I trust everyone to be on their best behavior? I'm speaking to you, Eddie."

"It's not my Edward you'll have to worry about, Katie. It's your own pride getting in the way of us all being ourselves."

I am upset with my mother for a moment, but then I know she is right, and I apologize. I don't want to put on airs or pretend that any of this is normal, as they will find out soon enough that my family, and myself included, are goofy. Eli accepts us with open arms, so why am I so judgmental?

"Dear Jesus,

Please heal my hardened heart that is prideful.
I only want to live in honesty and love.
Help me show my family the appreciation and kindness that they
show me and others.
And please, please help me convince my mother to leave her
camcorder at home, if that is Your will.

In Your name,
Amen."

"Tonight is Eli's outreach program for the church. It's his Bark Park Ministry. Would you all like to join us?" I look over to Edward who is lovingly gazing into my mother's eyes.

"Oh, doesn't that sound fun? Let me see if we brought Eddie's muzzle." My mother goes searching through my father's suitcase.

"We better bring my shin guards, just in case," my father mentions as she pulls the items out.

*****

"There's one place I need to stop before we go," I tell my mother from the back seat where I sit with both Dolly and Edward, each in their car seats and me in the middle.

"Okay, where to?"

I tell her the location, and my mother makes a swift and unexpected U-turn, now taking us in the correct direction, but I am rattled at the movement.

"Almost there, Katie."

I hadn't told her we had to get there in record time, but I let it go.

As we pull up to the Pup Street Bakery, I tell them I'll be back in a flash. "Do you guys want anything?" Neither Dolly nor Edward responds, but my father does.

"I'll take a glazed jelly doughnut."

I laugh but remember there is a doughnut shop next door. "No problem. What about you?"

My mother waves it off. "I'm fine. If I change my mind, I'll have a bite of his."

Knowing full well that means I need a half dozen doughnuts, I shut the car door behind me.

Stepping into the Pup Street Bakery first, I am overjoyed to see they've just put out a new collection of sports themed dog treats at a special price of $2/treat. I'll take an assortment of ten, please."

The baker nods, whistling away as he puts each one into small, individual bags so they won't crumble. I pay and thank him and slip over to the doughnut shop next door. I decide to just go all out and get doughnuts for everyone tonight, as my parents having traces of sugar and jelly around their mouths will give it away that they have treats in the car that they aren't sharing. And sharing is caring.

The doughnuts are beautiful at this store; each one has gourmet toppings and delectable flavors like maple cream, strawberry rhubarb, and raspberry custard. I could eat them all, and judging by the amount I end up getting, I know I'll need at least one more *Flab to Fab* workout class before the big day. The other option being that I skip eating a doughnut tonight, but where's the fun in that?

On my way out of the bakery, I notice a small selection of doughnut bites with plastic wedding ring toppers on them. I laugh and asked for a half dozen of them and leave with enough sugar to ensure my dentist can afford a new Rolex.

At six o'clock on Tuesday nights, we host a get together at the Bark Park. On Thursday nights, Eli hosts his youth group at his other church, and I would help there occasionally, but since it is a young men's group, I end up pushing around the coffee cart for all the different Bible studies that are happening throughout the building. It is an old schoolhouse and contains a multitude of rooms perfect for small groups, and I really admire the size and the attendance the church has, but it only makes me realize how much I value the friendships and fellowship from my own church.

While I didn't ask him to choose my church to attend on Sundays, I was so thankful when he offered because of the fellowship I had there. And with Eli's church being much, much larger, he felt he wouldn't be missed like I'd be from mine.

I meet Eli at the park at 5:45 since I am riding around with my mother, as we would normally drive there together. He has a few things he brings along with him weekly, such as the beautiful brochures he made comparing God's love and comfort to that of a pet, complete with color photos of Carter holding his squeaky toy and some vague images of him being held by Eli. He loves this kind of outreach, and while it is something that months ago you couldn't pay me to attend out of my own fears, awkwardness, and insecurity, being here has helped me grow in more ways than I'd ever imagined possible.

There are picnic tables set up near the "Pawrent" benches now, a new addition to the park, made possible by Eli's group making donations to the city for them and greatly helping us out so we can accommodate more people. This is by far the cleanest dog park in the area, and the quietest, with the road being blocked by a wooded area, so we are extremely fortunate the city was willing to improve upon it further.

When I arrive carrying two large boxes full of doughnuts, a small box of doughnut holes, and a bag of treats from the doggy bakery, he laughs and points to the box of coffee he'd just so happened to pick up from Beans N Greens. We are giggling at the coincidence when he opens the first box of doughnuts, eager to see what I picked out. I can't believe my eyes when we sees there isa bite taken from four of them.

"Katie, did you sample these?" He smirks at me, motioning to the powdered sugar around my mouth. "I guess I know which ones are ours." He picks up one of my least favorite flavors and bites into it, pouring himself some coffee into one of the dozen disposable cups he'd provided.

"Before everyone gets here, I want to tell you something." My words prompt Eli to have a startled look. "Don't worry, I'm sure it's nothing, but I've been having these weird dizzy spells. Probably from all of the excitement!"

His eyes looked around in concern. "And? When are you going to the doctor?" He sets his coffee down and takes both of my hands.

"Tomorrow, actually. At five. Right before our pizza date with my parents." I smile, trying to take the concern out of his face, but it doesn't work. Now I regret telling him.

Just then, he lowers his head in prayer, still holding onto my hands.

"Dear Heavenly Father,

I pray that my bride will be okay. I pray for wisdom for her doctor. And I pray for Your powerful peace to wash over us, that we may trust in You, and not worry about a thing. Our lives are in Your hands, and we trust You, Lord.

In Your name,

Amen."

I heard two voices echo Eli's "amen" as I turn to see my parents suddenly act like they weren't listening. I thank Eli and them all the same, taking him in for a hug. "Thank you for being here for me."

People started shuffling in while my parents get settled into one of the picnic tables, conveniently located where the coffee and treats are. We wait to open the doughnut holes until it is time to start, and Eli thinks it is so cute that I got those.

"I guess this is the last Bark Park Fellowship before the big day!" He puts his arm around me and kisses my head.

My parents gush at how exciting this time is for everyone.

"I never thought I'd see the day. . ." my mother loudly speaks to my father, who is hard of hearing on the side she is sitting on. Thankfully, she continues, ". . .that Katie would adopt a dog, come to the dog park, and get hit in the head by a frisbee thrown by her future husband. Does it get any better than that?"

We all laugh.

"That was the first time I'd thrown that frisbee, you know. I hadn't tossed one since I was a kid, and that one was exceptionally small. It was picked up by a gust of wind, I'm sure of it." He winks at me, and we turn to greet the people who are arriving.

"Oh, is that what happened?" I tease him back. "And what did you think when you saw it hit a woman?"

"When I saw it had hit a *beautiful* woman, I was certainly glad I threw it!"

Jenna and her husband, Gabriel, are first to arrive. They have a labrador retriever named Pumpkin, and while I always thought it was for her round shape from her overactive thyroid, Jenna has recently shown me a baby picture before Pumpkin had turned white, and she was a lovely orange hue. They each grab a donut, and Pumpkin chooses a treat from the bakery, and then they go to visit with my parents and meet my father.

Samantha and Mitchell will be absent tonight as Mitchell has inventory at PetWorld and couldn't get out of the shift, and Samantha is also covering a new adopter class. I think back to the night I attended my mandatory class and how the attention from Tommy had been both fun and upsetting. A week after that night, he quit the shelter and moved to Boston where the woman he was speaking to online lived. Samantha has since hired two wonderful people who are just as caring and attentive to the animals as she is, and I have started volunteering there as needed. I couldn't believe it myself when I agreed to it, but she was short of a few cat washers and groomers, neither job of which I have ever done professionally, but under the guise of volunteering, almost anything can be legit. I've since learned how to floss a cat's teeth, what color they like their nails painted, and which feather hair extensions double as their playtime. Thankfully, she hasn't needed me lately, as adoptions are increasing!

A few more people shuffle in with their dogs, and Micah and Carolyn are the last to arrive. They had been somewhat standoffish from Eli and me since they'd got together, which neither of us want, as we are truly happy for them both and think they make a great couple. But tonight, they are acting a little giggly and more secretive than usual, which I brush off as it's none of my business, and Carolyn and I don't have much more than an acquaintance relationship.

Now that the usuals are here, I open the box of doughnut holes, and Carolyn and Micah look at each other with wide eyes. "I thought these were perfect for the occasion." I push the box towards them, encouraging them to have one. "I know how each of you watches what you eat as well, so these little bit size treats are sure to do little havoc to your trim bods!"

They looked all around in wonder before each quietly grabbing one. What is up with that? We've all moved on—sure, Eli and Carolyn had a brief romance years ago (albeit serious), and Micah wanted to go on a date with me that one time—but all of that led them to each other, so what's up with how they are acting?

I shrug it off and will later ask Eli if he picked up on anything, but when I look over at him, and he is deep into a conversation with Gabriel and Ty, one of the young men from his other church who also attends this, I know he won't be picking up on too much.

Every time we meet, other people attending the dog park shuffle in and out, having natural conversations and asking questions. Sometimes we meet people who have great interest in coming to Three Maples or hearing more about the Lord and that is the best part of all this.

Once, there was a man who came to the park during one of our fellowship nights, and after he wandered over to us, we found out he'd just lost his dog to cancer. There wasn't a dry eye in the house. What started as him coming to the dog park because it was in his routine for so long, a routine that he felt he needed to continue right as we started our ministry, he was met with a fellowship group and new friends who welcomed him and reminded him of God's love. It was absolutely beautiful.

The group at the Bark Park begins to wind down as the dogs are getting tired of their treat fueled zoomies, and we are running very low on doughnuts. The evening dew has arrived on the grass, and Jenna's husband, Gabriel, slips when picking up after Pumpkin. It is one of those moments where you react with laughter, immediately stop laughing, repent, recite Bible verses until they get up, and you see they are not only fine, but also laughing, and now you are free to nearly wet your pants at their expense.

My eyes wander over in laughter to my mother, who looks rather serious, and I go to her. "Are you okay, mom?" I whisper, so as not to bring any attention to us.

She nods her head. "I was just remembering when I took you to the park as a child."

I sit down next to her, smiling as I wonder which time, as she reminds me of the instance.

Once, when my mother wanted to report suspicious activity, she flagged down a security guard across the street from the park we had been at. Right when I saw him, in my young, still-forming mind, I started singing the theme song from the show "Cops." The guard was so surprised, he made sure to give my mother's report a minute more than usual.

"So, you're telling me, this is a dog-free zone, but someone is breaking that rule, correct?"

"Yes, officer, that is correct. The sign on the corner clearly states NO DOGS ALLOWED. But the amount of dog... er, feces, tells me someone has been breaking that rule."

"That sign to me isn't very clear, ma'am. It looks like it says no skateboarding, smoking dogs allowed."

She looked back at the sign, agreeing with him. "Yes, the dog is skateboarding and smoking, but there's a big X over it, meaning don't do those things here."

"Don't do the three of them at once, absolutely. But separately? I'm no judge, but I think that sign is a little misleading,"

My mother huffed at the security guards words. "Sir, may I call you sir? Even if it was 'No skateboarding, smoking dogs allowed,' as you say, they still defecate the same, am I right?"

"Smokers are known to have very poor bowel movements, ma'am."

They continued to stare at one another in silence, when my newly forming lawful mind begged a question. "But unless the dog was smoking and surfing, is it really illegal?"

My mother threw her hands up and we left, moving locations of her "True Crime Book Time" group with other moms in the area to a different park.

As the night is winding down, we start packing up the boxes and Eli collects the recycling. Gabriel has recovered from his fall and is chatting with my parents as Jenna puts Pumpkin's leash back on. Though she is already wiped out from playtime, Jenna jokes that Gabriel will need to carry her to the car.

"So, have you seen anything like my case?"

My ears perk as I assume my mother is speaking, but it is my father, speaking to Gabriel.

"I'd love to spend some time with him. I'm working on a paper for my PhD, and this dog sounds like the perfect specimen to base my study around, if you don't mind?"

"That works for us fine. Edward and I will be driving back home next week, though. Do we have enough time?"

I hadn't seen my father this eager about anything in my lifetime.

"Yes—I was just going to say, these types of cases come up so rarely… It's worth rescheduling my other clients. I could even come by tomorrow. The only one I don't think I can move is Tally the Cockatiel. We've made so much progress in the last few months, but she really holds a grudge and starts cursing at everyone who passes by if I'm even five minutes late. We think she's spent some time around sailors. . . Or that's at least our working theory."

Gabriel is going to study Edward for his PhD? I can't think of anything closer to wonderland for a pet behaviorist.

Everyone says their goodbyes, and I send the last few doughnuts home with Eli, so he can have them for breakfast the next day.

"You won't believe it, but this is nowhere near as much sugar as my mom tried to give me this morning."

We laugh as I tell him about the maple syrup, and she pipes up after loading Edward and Dolly into their car seats.

"Katie used to eat JUST like that when she was a kid. How was I supposed to know she's 'healthy' now?"

"Your use of air quotes is offensive." I am cracking up as I say it.

"Just wait until we get our nails done—you'll be looking for an excuse to quote something."

Eli makes sure we all make it into the car and then waves us off. "I'll see you tomorrow for pizza at Katie's! And be sure to let me know if any other dizziness happens, or if you want me to attend tomorrow. Even just to sit in the waiting room. I can leave work early."

I thank him for his moral support. My parents say goodnight to him, and we drive down the road to the hotel where my father and Edward are staying. They happily say goodbye, and I open the back door, so I can move to the front seat, and my mother stops me.

"Katie, this might be my last chance to pretend you're still a child. Let me be the driver. In five minutes, we will be back at your apartment, and you'll be preparing to wed."

For a moment I think she is tearing up, but then it turns into full blown tears. "Are you okay?"
She nods and says yes. "I'm just so happy, Katie. This is everything I've ever wanted for you. A God-fearing husband, a full social life of friends. . . You have it all, and I couldn't be more thankful."

I get out of the car as we sit parked in the hotel lot still, and she steps out from behind the wheel, and we hug. Then, she promptly takes my spot in the back seat and asks if I will drive us back.

"I'm exhausted. I might not be able to watch all five episodes of *The Wedding Veil Killer* like I hoped."

Chapter 6
A Howling Good Time
Carolyn

Since I've been freed from the weight of sin, almost instantaneously when I sin, I feel a little nudge in my heart. This is especially true when my biggest crutch comes out: judging others, for anything and everything. I know that meeting Micah at the airport will spark much temptation to judge strangers for their attire that I deem inappropriate for public wear, so I say a prayer before I go into the terminal.

"Lord, please continue to soften my heart. I am so far from perfect, and we all fall so short of your glory. You are the only judge of this world, and I pray to only see the best in others that I may be a steward of Your love, kindness, and grace."

Micah taps on the window as I am praying, and my heart skips a beat. I am so excited to come to Wyoming. I haven't left the Pacific Northwest in years. I didn't want to look like a tourist, but I also didn't want to stick out like a sore thumb, so in lieu of tennis shoes, I purchased a pair of floral western boots. They have a slender toe, as opposed to a round or square, so I immediately ask Micah if they are the right style for me to fit in.

"You look gorgeous in them; you'll blend right in with the wranglers." He kisses me, lingering for a moment longer than I expect, instantly reminding me of the physical chemistry that awaits.

If he asks me to marry him right now, in this parking lot of the airport, I will say yes. But I'd also wait another year, two, or as long as it takes, because I truly love this guy.

He gathers my luggage from the backseat of my car and doesn't say anything about the number of bags. I brought seven pieces of luggage, but they all vary in size, and Micah doesn't know, but some of them are full of presents for his family. I went out last night and got a few souvenirs, locally made honeys, jellies, and some of my favorite chocolates. I also had an 8x10 photo of Micah which I framed for their home. Micah, my perfect match, will be thrilled that I did this, and I can't wait to meet his family. They are my future.

The plane touches down and it is country for as far as I can see. I knew Micah grew up quite rural, only moving to the Pacific Northwest for college and falling in love with the rain, but I am surprised at how dry and arid the climate is out here, though he always told me it is. "Your skin cracks the moment you get off the plane," he would joke. It's quite the opposite of where we live, as the humidity and rain is never ending, keeping our skin quite supple.

His parents are able to come out onto the tarmac and greet us while we wait for our luggage to come via cart, instead of inside on the belt like other airports.

"There they are!" Micah runs over to them, and I quickly follow.

His mother has his beautiful eyes; his father his perfect hair, and the blend of them together makes his bubbling personality. The joy these two parents exude is instantly contagious.

"Caroline, bring it here!"

His mother takes me in for a deep hug, and his father next. They smell like fresh air and feel like home. We chat excitedly, and Micah signals his father to help with the bags, and we walk the short distance to their truck, parked on the curb out front. There are no toll booths or parking meters here at this wide-open airport, and on the drive home, they tell me where the fun restaurants are and the small shopping center or the local grocery store that doubles as a teenager hangout. It is a little gem of a place, hidden away from the world in row after row of mountain ranges. While I find the town vacant of much, I also find the sky void of clouds, the landscape free from skyscrapers, and a multitude of picturesque chapels surrounded by open fields that colorful horses roam. I don't mean to do it, but upon seeing that particular church, the one I know is the one I want to marry in, I gasp.

Micah takes my hand. "I know," he says, and we look into each other's eyes, and he kisses my hand. His parents, obviously aware of what is transpiring, smile at one another.

After about fifteen minutes in the car, we turn down a long, dirt road that has a large archway entrance. *Two Pines Ranch* is scrawled on the top, burned into a wooden sign. "Here we are. Home."

Micah is known for his surges of energy, as I playfully refer to them as the "zoomies" like dogs get, and I can tell it is happening now. As soon as his dad puts the truck into park, he jumps out the door, running around to my side to open the door. I take his hand as I step down, gasping again at my beautiful surroundings.

There is a sprawling horse corral with dozens of beautiful manes running freely. Several log cabins, varying in sizes, are planted along a line, as Micah explains to me that they are guest quarters and ranch hands. The main home is both log and stone and has a weathered tin roof.

"I bet it sounds beautiful when it rains here." I dream of the sound lulling me to sleep as my feet are planted into a part of the earth I have only just met, but feel like I've always known, or always have yearned for. This place, in its high desert climate, its mountainous views, its wildness... This is where I want to be.

*****

After Micah's mom shows me to my room, a beautiful guest room right next to theirs, I find myself already wishing this trip will never end. She immediately gives me a tour of their rustic abode when we walk in, while the men take care of the luggage in the truck. I can't wait to dive into the baby pictures of Micah on the mantle, but first, she wants to show me the finicky shower handle and where the light switches are. I admit, I feel like she is distracting me for something else, but I love it all the same.

Her beautiful home is decorated tastefully and surprisingly modern. Upon seeing it outside, I assumed the home would have antlers and taxidermy everywhere on the walls, but in place of skulls there are fresh flowers. Beautiful oil paintings depicting scenes of the west scatter the walls, and the house is spotless and free from clutter. She leaves me alone to get settled, and I can't wait to do so. I never want to leave.

I freshen up in the hallway bathroom before going back downstairs. I will save the gifts I bought for them until tomorrow, as his parents tell us they are having a barbeque reception with all of their family coming over soon. I'm not just meeting Micah's parents, but his aunts, uncles, cousins, neighbors, childhood friends and to my surprise, his parents' pastor. I had unfairly assumed that since Micah was a new Christian, that his parents were non-believers, but I was wrong. And more and more these days, I love being wrong.

When I return back downstairs, with a fresh dusting of powder on my face and my hair brushed, no one is there. I check the time: *4:07.* Could the barbeque already be happening? I suppose it could, so I go through the kitchen and look out the window, but I can't see anything from this angle. It certainly smells like someone is cooking, so I leave out the back kitchen door, my floral cowboy boots crunching through a path of freshly-laid gravel.

As I turn the corner, behind the house is a meticulous backyard, complete with a creek running through it. I am shocked to see that thirty or forty people are here, and I hadn't heard any sign of them while I was inside. I can see the top of a picturesque gazebo with a view of the frosted mountain range through the amount of people. I look around for Micah, not seeing him right away, when Micah's father sees me and calls me over.

He hollers out to his family, "Everyone, this is the lovely Carolyn that our beloved son has brought home!"

I laugh at the awkwardness of everyone looking in my direction, until I realize they are joyfully cheering me on to walk into the crowd.

"Come here, Carolyn," Micah's dad hollers back over to me, waving me to come his way. The crowd opens up, leading me to the gazebo.

Micah stands inside and holds his hand out for me to join him. I don't know what this is about, but I hope it is something. Everything is just so beautiful and feels so right.

Micah gets down on one knee, and I say, "Yes" before he even pulls out the box.

"You all hear that? She doesn't need a ring!"

Normally, a comment of that nature would bother or embarrass me, but in embracing God's grace, I am learning to love people for what they are, so I do something out of my character and very publicly reply, "Well, don't go *that* far, buddy!"

Everyone laughs, especially Micah. He proceeds to open a ring box to unveil a beautiful diamond ring on a silver band. "Carolyn, there is nothing in this world that would make me happier than you becoming my forever date to the movies. Will you marry me?"

"Yes! Yes, a thousand times over!" It's official. I am surrounded by my new family, and I can't wait to meet all of them, after I kiss my fiancé.

*****

The rest of the day is filled with well wishes and hugs from my future family. It turns out, this has all been planned by Micah, and I couldn't be happier. I love everything he did for me.

As we are winding down the night, his maternal grandmother asks us when we plan on marrying. "I don't want to put any pressure on you kids, but you know this is just all so exciting for us old folks out here."

She is an absolute peach of a woman, from what I can tell and from the beautiful stories Micah has told me. I look at Micah to see what he says.

"I hope soon!" Micah beams.

The butterflies in my stomach do a flip. I hope soon, too. In fact, I'll do it right now if that pastor comes to the gazebo.

She tells us goodnight and kisses us both on the cheek. His grandparents live in a small cabin on the property, both sets, and it's about as adorable as it sounds. They are a very close family, which couldn't be any more different than my own, as I have a few scattered relatives but nothing substantial; no one I could call if I needed something or had an emergency. I was adopted as a little girl, but my adoptive parents were abusive, and I've subsequently cut them out of my life. That's something I've worked through extensively, and I know a major reason why I battle with judging others, is because of the treatment I endured all of my life. I've looked for my birth parents off and on, but records overseas are hard to navigate, plus with the language barrier, almost impossible. While I hope one day to find out more about my roots, I'm happy to place new ones right here.

As she leaves, Micah looks at me. "I have a proposal for you." He takes both of my hands in his.

"You already did propose, remember?" I hold up my beautiful sparkling ring to jog his memory.

He smiles and nods. "How could I forget the best day of my life... so far? My next proposal is for our wedding date."

My heart leaps. "Yes? And what's that?"

"That little chapel we drove by on the way in; that's my parent's church, and their pastor has agreed to marry us... Anytime."

I am speechless. That chapel is the dream venue for my wedding, and I don't even care what it looks like inside. It's such a beautiful spot to put our vows into words and commit to one another for the rest of our days. "I'd love that... and I am also ready, you know, anytime." I dance around my words, not out of embarrassment or fear, but it just feels good to play in this moment, to hold the words in my mouth before I say them, to relish in each second.

"How about tomorrow?"

Chapter 7
Dog Spelled Backwards
Katie

The days start to fill up with happenings at lightning speed. Just this week alone we have several fun things like our nail appointments, my final dress fitting, and now spray tans, speaking of which my mother has boldly scheduled two separate appointments, one this week and one the day before my wedding. When I ask her why she dared to do it so close to the wedding, she shakes her head. With a little over a week left, I'm not sure how long the tan will last, but I'm not sure I want to double up, either.

"It will be fresh and not streaky, as they get sometimes." She accentuates her words with her hands, showing off her new nails.

"Streaky? Why would I want to have *streaks* anywhere on my body... Ever?" I make a question gesture with my hands, also not able to get enough of my own acrylics.

"That's why you take that high powered exfoliant with you, for when it starts to break up and dissolve, you can scrub it off." She pretends to scrub her arms with her nails like daggers going in every direction.

"That *'scrub'* you got me is *illegal* in some countries. I don't need to be losing skin over this," really emphasizing my air quotes, as now we are in an unspoken competition over whose nails are *better.*

"Don't be such a wimp; the skin will come back, and it will be softer." My mother gestures for me to stop with jazz hands but is hysterically laughing as I hand her the scrub and dramatically point my nail at the label.

"Yep, you are right. It says right here it's only *allowed* in the great USA."

She shrugs, putting her hands down and admiring the shape of her new claws. When we sit down at the salon, I show my nail tech a photo of a classic white tip set, and my mother just says one simple word to which they noddingly reply, "Chiclets."

"Where did you find the scrub, anyway?" I take a sip of water from my glass.

"At the discount store, well, they have a new *discount bin.*"

I spit out my water all over, nearly choking from laughter.

As the time gets closer to my doctor's appointment, I start to feel the alarm bells of worry go off in my head. "What if" comes and goes, several times, to the point where there is nothing else I can do but step away and go spend some time reading the Bible.

Katie's Biblical Application

Do not be anxious about anything, but in every situation, by prayer and petition, with thanksgiving, present your requests to God. And the peace of God, which transcends all understanding, will guard your hearts and your minds in Christ Jesus. —Philippians 4:6–7

When it is time to leave, I lock the door to my apartment. Marge is outside but just gives us a polite wave. Marge finally pipes up, "Good luck!" and I thank her. Of course, she knows what is going on, but I am thankful that my mother has made a friend here.

When we get to the car, I hand her the keys. "Why don't you drive? Considering you know just where it is and all." I laughed, but it doesn't reach my eyes. She nods and takes the keys.

It is a lovely, new, modern clinic with lots of aesthetic and calming decor. Large, leafy plants sit in muted colored planters in corners. Instead of sterile chairs, there are plush, velvet couches with overstuffed throw pillows. A coffee station is in the lobby, offering every type of drink you can imagine, while the tables don a plethora of candies and mints. When it is my turn to speak to the receptionist, she politely recommends that I not have any of the sweets, so it won't interfere with my blood test. My hands feel shaky at the thought of it.

Dr. Brand's assistant calls me back promptly at 4:59, takes my vitals, and to my amazement, it doesn't take an extra hour for the doctor herself to walk in. She waltzes in a moment later.

After our cordial greeting, I explain again my symptoms, and she writes it all down on her clipboard, and fires off a round of questions about my general health and experiences. Her assistant comes back in and gets a vial of blood.

"From this, I am going to find out a lot of things, and most importantly, what other things we need to test. For instance, your dizziness could be caused by a hormonal issue. I've seen that quite a bit in women your age. In any case, the blood test will reveal anything else. We have a lab in house, so I'll know the results by tomorrow."

All said and done, I am out of there in fifteen minutes, but I feel that I am in great hands. The second we get into the car, I text Eli a short summary.

Just left the doctor's office. It might be a hormonal problem causing dizziness. The good news is, my results will be back tomorrow!

Eli replies nearly immediately.

Ah, great news to get word so fast! I am just leaving the pizza parlor. Will be with you in ten minutes for a fun night!

My father and Edward come over and Eli joins us. We order pizzas and sit around my table, usually reserved for puzzling. In fact, I am in the middle of a puzzle right now despite everything else going on, so our plates just sit right on top, but my father still manages to put a few pieces together.

"I'm so glad to hear you'll be taking Katie skiing, Eli. I've always wanted her to learn."

My mother and I go silent as we watch our two men converse.

"Ahh, yes. Katie tells me you used to race a little back in the day?" Eli takes a bite of his supreme pizza after dipping it in extra marinara.

"You bet I did. Won a few, too. That was the 70's. Let's just say there was nothing better than skiing and disco. Sometimes, simultaneously."

The whole table went silent, and for once, even my mother is without words.

"So, uh, Eli? How was work today?" I stammer out a question as best I can, desperate to redirect before my dad starts reminiscing about lava lamps.

"It's fine." His tone seems very *wrong,* but I don't want to pry.

Thankfully, my mother does. "What do you mean, Eli? Is everything okay with Dr. McArty?"

Eli shrugs and then relents. "Just today, there has been talk about him retiring soon—as in *very soon.* I knew he was considering it, but after that patient came in with drastically different sized feet, and the doc accidentally made the small one large rather than the large one small, we just haven't quite recovered, client wise."

"Yes, I think I heard about that a long time ago; I'd forgotten until now. 'The Case of the Disproportionate Digits' as they said in the paper. Terribly sorry about that. What will you do if he closes?"

"Well, today on my lunch break, I applied at a handful of other clinics that might be looking for an x-ray technician. But there is something I think we should all discuss."

Eli takes a drink of his Pepsi while my mother and I wait in anticipation, as my father lets out an 'Ah-ha!' as he places another puzzle piece.

"What's that, Eli?" I ask, not sure I like the sound of this.

"There aren't many clinics around here hiring, and then I started to think about our future. I know we are both here right now because of our jobs, and I know you love your job, and Frank is the best guy ever to work for. But do we want to live here forever?"

The thought hadn't crossed my mind until now. "I honestly have no idea. What did you have in mind?"

"Have you thought about moving closer to mommy?" My mother perked up in her chair, and Eli laughs.

While he is nodding, I have a strange mix of emotions come over me.

"Actually, the job opportunities out west are less than the city, but the cost of living and home prices are too. Katie, we don't have to go anywhere if you don't want to, but I thought we could openly discuss it as a family."

My mother smiles ear to ear when he says that.

"Imagine us owning a home with a big back yard for Carter and Dolly to play in? We could start a miniature poodle training center if we wanted."

"What would you train them for? Hand-to-hand combat?" My father rejoins the conversation briefly, before returning to the puzzle pieces.

"I was thinking more about manners and behavior lessons. But that's just one of my many ideas. I just love working with dogs."

Hearing Eli speak from the heart makes me deeply contemplate the possibility of us living elsewhere. Yes, we have a wonderful church family here, but they can continue without us, and we could always visit, right? Eli's Bark Park ministry could be headed up by one of the other people who attend, such as Mitchell or Samantha. Next, the thought of leaving my first real friends here, Judy, Jenna, and Samantha, makes me feel sad. But knowing I will be starting my life with Eli soon resolves it.

"Other than our church friends, there's nothing tying us down here, is there? I enjoy my job but could find another. Certainly, I would miss Judy, Samantha, Jenna... But I mean, we could still visit, right?"

My mom is now clapping her hands together and goes to the living room where out of the corner of my eye, I swear she does a cartwheel. But I am too busy focusing on Eli to see for sure.

"Thank you for having an open mind! We can discuss it further over the next few weeks. Thankfully, we still have two months left on your lease to really decide, and even if we haven't, we can always convert it to month-to-month until we do. Maybe we can take a little road trip in the weeks after our honeymoon and check a few places out?"

The thought of not one, but two fun trips makes me want to join my mother in the gymnastics gym that is my living room, but I keep it together for the sake of not scaring Dolly.

"I'd love to!" I throw my arms around his neck and rest my head on his shoulder.

"Hey, Eli, what do your parents do for a living?" my father chirps up, now moved on from the puzzling and pouring himself a root beer.

"My father is a chemical salesman, and my mother is a psychologist."

My father huffs, pauses, and then bursts out in maniacal laughter.

"And she's about to meet two new patients," I whisper to Eli as we look over to my parents in amazement.

Eli goes back to his place after dinner, and mother decides to go back to the hotel with my father.

"It's not that I don't want to be on your couch, Katie. But my sciatica is acting up from those cartwheels. I still got it, that's for sure, but my hips don't lie. Something is out. I'll be back in the morning."

"That's okay. Things have been so chaotic; it will be good for Dolly and me to have the place to ourselves. Besides, my puzzle needs to be completed so I can put it away." I look over at the progress my father made while we were enjoying our pizza, and I am really impressed.

After they leave, I am able to wind down and relax for the first time since my mother has arrived. I love having her here, but it feels great to clean up the apartment and be able to watch a television show without it involving any crime. After I run the vacuum cleaner while holding Dolly so she won't feel afraid, I look in the bag and laugh at the hundreds of popcorn kernels. "What in the world, Dolly? Where did all this come from? I'm glad you didn't eat them." And I am glad, because even though we have successfully found a new veterinarian, I'm not keen on the idea of needing any emergency care.

Our new vet was recommended to us by my neighbor, Patricia. She takes Mr. Twinkles to see Dr. Rally at Maple Hills Pet Hospital. "She's the only one I trust with my furbabies, Katie. You've got to go see her. And her prices are very reasonable."

The *she* was all I needed to hear before I agreed. I'm not against seeing a male veterinarian again, but after Dr. Wylons, I think a break was necessary. Besides, I'm an engaged woman now and don't want to drudge up the past.

The thoughts of Dr. Wylons—err, Taylor, makes me suddenly curious, so after Dolly and I get settled on the couch, I grab my laptop from the coffee table and do a quick search on social media. His profile comes up easily, as his full name has and always read, *Dr. Taylor Wylons, DVM,* so there's no mistaking him, but it's his profile picture that throws me off. It's a photo of him and his secretary, Patty. I thought back to the one and only time I ever met her, with her long clacking nails pounding away on the keyboard; had she noy been completely disturbed when he asked me out? Yes, and hadn't she said he had dated her sister and stood her up? I couldn't quite recall all the details, but I shrug it off; it is none of my business. And yet, I don't let that stop me from scrolling through his recent posts.

From the looks of it, they've recently been on a tropical vacation, but I can't tell where. In an album of dozens of photos that Patty has posted but tagged Taylor in, the scenery pics are mostly of them, until I reach the end, that is. Suddenly, the pictures take a turn to a candlelit beach dinner. It looks beautiful and quite romantic. There are tiki torches lit around them in a wide heart shape and a pale pink rug that leads to their table through the sand. Patty has captured every moment of this dinner, and my jaw drops at the end: a sole picture of Taylor, holding up the back of his left hand, accentuating a ring on his finger. The caption reads, "*He said yes.*"

The idea of Patty, just a few months ago, proposing to a man that she had warned me about surprised me, but apparently, she's worked those things out. I can't call myself my mother's daughter if I don't read the comments, so I give those a quick scroll, unsurprised at the amount of them, but truthfully only looking for one name: Clarissa, the swimsuit model whom he was enamored with during our dinner date, if you could even call it that, to the point that he didn't notice my stepping out moments later.

Sure enough, she is in there with the comment, "Wow, I can't believe it. Really? Congratulations..."

Since she's a married woman, I am a little surprised at her apparent shock, but then again, with how they behaved around each other, I guess I'm not.

Of course, hers is the only comment that Taylor acknowledged with a reply: "We have to get together so I can tell you all about my trip to the islands."

His response makes me feel squirmy. Having seen them interact, I felt icky for Patty, but maybe to her, that wasn't a big deal. It sure was a deal breaker for me.

I close the laptop and set it on my coffee table while I absently grab the remote control, going straight for a made-for-television movie channel. There are a lot of things I need to think about in the next few weeks; moving to another place is now a pretty heavy decision. Do I want to leave all of this behind? I look around my apartment at the little mementos I've collected: the seashell picture frame, holding a treasured memory of a day at the beach with my parents; a maroon woven rug I found at an antique store in my hometown; knickknacks from friends or shopping trips from college and before, none of which were even from here. Other than my church life, I haven't ever set down roots in this rainy town. It was as if God only placed me here so I could meet Eli and Dolly, and for that, I am at peace.

I readjust on the couch and feel something poking me in the lower back. "Hold on, Dolly." I move her over so I can fish it out. I am shocked as I pull out a giant Sherlock Holmes style magnifying glass that my mother must have misplaced. Checking the time, it is past 10 p.m., and both are probably already asleep, so I assume she won't be needing it tonight, and I put it on the coffee table for her. Who knows what other treasures lay hidden inside this couch, but I am too tired to look, and the moment I turn up the volume as the movie starts, my eyes slam shut.

It is past 2 a.m. when I wake up on the couch, the movie finished and now an infomercial is playing on a loop. There are two women smiling ear to ear, while their eyes look like they'd just reminded someone to put the toilet seat down. At first, I can't tell what they are selling. All the bottom of the screen says is "Comes in a 24-karat gold container." I turn up the volume to see what they are talking about, and the camera keeps zooming in on their perfect, dazzling teeth. "Dolly, I need this, whatever it is." It's not that my teeth are yellow, but they aren't sparkling white either.

Finally, the screen changes to a picture of the product. "'Grin & Bare It' Slip-on veneers!"

"What now?" Dolly looks up at me. I know it is past our bedtime, but I had no idea this existed before today. . .

"Now made without toxic chemicals! Guaranteed to love this new formulation of materials as it has no taste or smell. But don't worry—it's still completely non-stick!"

A small paragraph of text appears at the bottom of the screen: "Our lawyers said we must disclose that the previous version of this product is in a class-action lawsuit for causing side effects."

"Okay, it's bedtime Dolly. I think we've seen enough." I turn off the television and am inspired to do a very thorough oral hygiene regime before dozing off finally in my bed, after tucking Dolly into hers nearby.

"Tired of coffee-stained teeth ruining your morning selfie? Sick of spending a fortune on expensive dental work? Introducing the revolutionary solution: 'Grin & Bare It' Slip-On Veneers! Say goodbye to inconvenient dental appointments and hello to instant perfection!"

I'm not sure where the voice is coming from, but suddenly, I am standing outside of a coffee shop when I make eye contact with a man walking down the street with a dazzling smile.

He stops and turns to me, "Why wait for the perfect smile when you don't have to? 'Grin & Bare It,' because life is too short to take dental health seriously."

I looked to the left and right of me, expecting to see a camera crew, but it's just my mother with her camcorder. "Katie, his teeth look dazzling, don't you think? You'd never know they were slip-ons, am I right?"

I lean in a little closer as the man is still posing, smiling in a way that all his upper teeth can be seen. "I—I don't know. I mean, I can't see any spaces in between them. That's kind of a dead giveaway, I'd say."

Abruptly, the background music stops playing, the cars that are moseying come to a screeching halt, and the patrons and workers inside the coffee shop freeze. The man's smile fades, but his mouth is still ajar when I realize his lips are stuck on his teeth, like how it happens to dogs when their head is out the car window too long. This man has been walking around showing off his grill during the entire infomercial, and now there's no moisture left in that region.

"Little side effects of the veneers, I'm afraid."

After he speaks, the voiceover from earlier is heard again.

"Side effects include dry mouth, tooth decay, painful gums, painful urination, moodiness, headaches, lockjaw, jaw discomfort, cannibalism, early onset prune requirement and chronic fatigue, gas, and bloating. All at once."

The next morning, I awake to a bird chirping outside and when I open my eyes, it looks later than I had intended. Peeking over at Dolly, she's still snoring gently, so I relax again and reach for my phone on my bedside table and see that it's nearly 10 a.m., and most importantly, no missed calls from my mother. She must be sleeping in, too. I am thrilled to receive my usual morning texts from Eli.

I opened my text messages to see there are more than one, so I scroll up and read them in order:

Good morning to my favorite ladies (bride emoji) (dog emoji) (detective emoji) Just a few more sleeps until you are mine forever. Gee, I think that came out wrong. (face palm emoji)
I meant that you would be mine forever. Of course, Dolly will be ours.
And your mother will be in my life forever too, ha-ha. Okay, I guess I did mean it that way.

After replying to his texts with some laughter and acknowledgement that I know what he means, and that he is stuck with all of us forever, a thrill of anticipation runs through me, picking up my heart rate from slumber to running a marathon. He sends me a quick reply of a heart, as he is at work, so usually I get random texts throughout the day when he isn't with a client. I can't wait to become his wife! With no urgency to get up, I retrieve my Bible from the drawer along with my journal and pens, and I read what the Lord reveals to me.

A while later, Dolly and I get up and shuffle around the apartment, relishing the quiet. A crazy thought crosses my brain: What will Eli be like to live with? He and I have similar work schedules, that is, until we don't. His uncertainty about his current position does cause a little nervousness in my mind, until I remember that it's all in God's hands. There is nothing that surprises the Lord, and since all our days are written out in His book of life, and all things work together for His purpose, what is there to ever worry about? Floating on the high of God's love and will for us, I decide to text Eli and see how his work is going today, and he replies within just a few minutes:

Not too good. Dr. McArty just told us the building is for sale. We aren't going anywhere just yet, but it's happening. I'm glad we could all talk last night; it feels a little less scary going into this knowing we have options. I'm about to start doing some x-rays, and I will call you at lunch and see what you ladies are up to!

I think about my reflections of last night and say another prayer for the idea.

"Dear Jesus,
If it is Your will for us to embark on a new adventure,
Whatever that may be, please light the path and we will follow.

In your name,
Amen."

I've been thinking about it quite a bit and praying that the right doors will open. I'll go anywhere with you, Eli Skatey.

I responded to his text and my cheeks flushed as I hit "send."

After getting Dolly out of her cozy bed so she can use her grass pad on the patio, I tighten my bathrobe as I feel the chill in the air. "Are we ever going to get Spring?" I ask myself, out loud, rhetorically.

"No," a voice answers back.

I put my hand over my mouth to keep myself from screaming in fear, but seeing Dolly wiggle back inside in fright, I realize I had screamed anyway.

"Sorry. . . I, uh, didn't mean to scare you," the voice calls back again, and for the second time, I have no idea where it is coming from.

"Who—where are you?" I am now standing inside my second story apartment but hold the handle on my sliding door with all my might, so I can shut it in a heartbeat if the killer rappels down the building.

"I'm over here."

I look all around but only see a pigeon on the neighbor's railing. It *is* staring at me with beady eyes, but I still don't see anyone. I slide the door closed and lock it, just to be safe.

Where is my mother when I need her? She would be all over this situation. I decide I better give the sleuth a call and see where she is.

"Hi, Katie," she answers on the first ring. "I was just about to call you. I was handling some business this morning with my crime team- anyway. Today is our first spray tan appointment, but I am thinking it might not look as good if we layer it like that, considering the wedding is a week away, so I canceled it. The last time I layered spray tans, all around my hairline I started to look like Tupperware that's stained with spaghetti sauce. I thought instead, we could go see Samantha and help her find her foster dog families."

Thoughts about my wedding being here in seven days sent shockwaves down my spine. "Yes, that sounds great, and I totally agree with your decision. I will call Samantha right now and see if today works for her."

"Great. I'll be over soon to get you since I have Dolly's car seat."

"Okay, give me about thirty minutes, will you? I just woke up," I admit, "and it's been a weird one so far." I can't remember the last time I slept in, but maybe I'm just feeling groggy.

"Whew, you must have needed it. I'm in no rush, Katie. Eddie really wants me around, I can tell. Why don't we take it easy this morning then, and you call me when you're ready?"

"That sounds great. Thank you." I hang up the phone and casually stroll to my kitchen to make a fresh pot of coffee. There are a few things I need to pick up today as well, especially since tonight's event is dinner with Eli's parents. And my parents will be meeting his parents for the first time, in person, anyway. It sounds like my mother and his have been in contact for quite some time. Sheesh.

I take back up the cleaning I started last night and wipe down all the surfaces in the kitchen, living room, and everything that's exposed around the puzzle. But I make the horrible mistake of letting my eyes see the puzzle while I'm trying to be productive, so I get roped into putting a few pieces together. After five minutes, I work up the will to keep moving and take my cleaning supplies into my room and bathroom where I continue tidying up.

Once back in the kitchen, I'm putting a few tea mugs into the sink when I notice my virtual assistant is still unplugged. Just for the heck of it, I plug it back in. For as much as I used to rely on this thing, I sure left it in the dust the moment I got Dolly.

"Virtual assistant, what's the best thing to take to dinner at your future in-laws house?" I know I need to hit up the store today to replenish a few things, especially for the dogs, but I have no idea what to take to his parents' house tonight.

Consider taking with you a conversation starter. Something to break the ice. Rubber chickens are known for their ability to bring humor into any situation, and guests in many cultures find such absurdities a gesture of goodwill.

One minute, I'm assuming robots will take over the world at any moment, and the next... "Virtual assistant: I am thinking more on the lines of an appetizer or punch."

Filling a rubber chicken with water and then freezing it for six hours will provide the ice for a punch in the most hysterical way. The receiving end of such a gift will never forget the experience.

I'm sure his psychologist's mother will never forget it — yeah, it's right about that!

I take my time getting ready, and it feels good to not be flying around at high speed today. I realize I undervalued how much I require a rest day now and then and consider calling my mother back when Samantha calls. I have my hair in a towel while I do my makeup, so I put her on speaker phone.

"Good morning! Are your ears burning? My mother was just asking if we could meet with you today." My voice is still a little scratchy from sleeping in.

"Aww, yes, that would be perfect! I was calling about that. I've been praying about it, and I have a couple that I really, really feel good about. I called them this morning to see when they could come in, and they said today would work best since they are both off work today. But Katie, there's something you should know."

"Oh? What is it?"

"It's Micah and Carolyn. But there's more."

I gasp, not out of shock as they made a lovely couple, but more out of coincidence. Still, I can't figure out logistically how that will work, since we know he lives in a studio apartment, and Carolyn with her parents.

"They got married last weekend at a chapel in his hometown, someplace in Wyoming."

I am floored—more so that we are only just hearing about it. Now, the apprehension of the bridal doughnut holes makes more sense, but I still am not sure why they didn't tell us. "That's wonderful news. I'm so happy for them!"

"I am too. They seem to be the perfect pair since the moment they met. So, since I've already picked the couple, do you still want to come in today? Or, if you're up for it, I am down one cat groomer."

Snickering, I agree to her terms since going into Newtown is the only thing my mother and I have plans for today. Surely, I can be of some use and get a few kitties looking better for their future homes.

"Great. I look forward to seeing you two gals soon!"

Samantha hangs up the phone, and I text my mother the new plans.

Samantha needs our help today at the shelter doing a few grooming duties with the cats if you are up to it? (cat emoji)
(typing...)
(typing...)
Get the catwalk ready, because those felines will be strutting their stuff when I'm done with them.

If there is any trait at all I wish I'd inherited from my mother, it is the belief that she could do anything. Whether or not she could, was another story entirely; but fake it until you make it, right? Like that time we went to the indoor surfing studio because I'm deathly afraid of sharks, and my mother wanted to see what she looked like in a wetsuit; it was an hour-long lesson before we even touched the water, but my mother declined the instruction, saying she knew just what to do. After signing the waivers, she held onto a rope from the base of the equipment to steady herself. She was doing well until they told us that now they would turn on the water. As my mother became airborne, still holding the rope as her legs went up behind her, I'd never seen grown men run so fast from a woman in my life until that point. I can see now how they thought she was going to land on them, as she could have, and at least that would have been a softer hit than the tile floor of where she really landed.

That night in the emergency room, she recalled her first day on a surfboard:

"What do you mean, your 'first' day? As in, you'd like to do that again?" I squint my eyes at her in disbelief, but with her head wrapped up in gauze, she can't tell. The only part of her body still exposed is her right hand.

"Katie, be a dear and hand me the television remote, will you?"

She points to a side table. How she saw it, I'll never know.

"But your eyes are covered."

I put it in her hand anyway and watch as she expertly works the remote that is quite different from the one we have at home, landing the channel on Dateline just as it starts. Sighing, I make myself comfortable in the chair next to her as the "Case of the Missing Mall Walker" starts playing.

"I remember this case. I think she ran off and started a new life with one of the kiosk workers selling hair straighteners."

After a busy morning around the house, I realize just how far gone my apartment got over the last week. It takes a few hours to get it straightened out. But finally, it is done. The apartment is thoroughly cooked, a light lunch is cleaned, the dishes are paid, and the bills are washed, so I call my mother and say that I am ready for her to come pick me up.

We arrive at Newtown as Samantha is meeting with Carolyn and Micah, and the first thing I do is look at their ring fingers to confirm what I already know. I didn't mean to be so obvious, and I feel a little shameful as their eyes immediately catch mine, revealing they know that I know their secret. *Dang.* I then look away as quickly as I can, not mentioning a thing and hoping it will all just fizzle out when Carolyn pipes up.

"Katie."

She walks over to me and my mother as we are walking to the grooming room, which is nothing more than a giant sink and a flat table. They are severely lacking in accessories, but I have my suspicions that my mother came prepared.

"Hey, Carolyn," I say casually, "how do you do?" I don't make eye contact for long, still hiding from my embarrassment. She holds her hand out to me, which at first, I instinctively take in mine, thinking this is the playground, and we are five years old, playing a game of Red Rover.

"Red rover, red rover, send Tara right over." A moment later, a red-headed six-year-old with the speed of a lumbering elephant is coming right towards me with the intention of breaking the hand-holding chain I have with little Suzy. I can't bear the suspense and am not sure my plastic watch will sustain the force of Tara bursting through our arms, so I wiggle out of Suzy's grip right before, losing the game to my chains' disgust.

I shivered at the memory as Carolyn releases the tight grip I have on her hand. "Oh, sorry Carolyn. I was having an out of body experience."

Both Carolyn and my mother look at me with wide eyes, and I realize I said that out loud.

"It's. . . okay, I guess. Anyway. . . I just wanted to tell you the news. We were going to wait until this weekend at church to announce it, but I think the cat's already out of the bag since Samantha's chosen us for the dogs. Micah and I are married."

Before I can congratulate her, my mother comes over with one of those eye spectacles, the magnifying kind, and is doing a three-point-inspection on the ring that Carolyn is holding up on her finger.

"Oh, my word. It's flawless! Truly timeless. Is it a family piece?" my mother asks as she takes her eyepiece off, revealing it is attached to a chain she wears around her neck.

Carolyn smiles, nodding. "Yes, it was his grandmother's ring. Micah coordinated the whole thing; I didn't even know he had it until he pulled it out of his pocket. We decided to elope then and there. Oh, it's such a dream out west, and being married to my guy is everything I could've hoped for."

"What a touching moment, Carolyn. I'm so happy for you both, and I wish you both a lifetime of happiness."

We both hug her, and she goes back to the front where Samantha is just finishing up the paperwork she had for them. My mother and I return to the sinks to see what we have for supplies, and then we hear two little barks coming from the front again. I peer around the corner and see the most charming Chihuahuas I have ever seen. One has longer hair, which is in two pigtails with bows; the other has a smooth coat. Both are tan with some other spots.

My heart leaps when I see them, just as it did when I met Dolly for the first time. And I begin to wonder: *Is there room in my heart for more furbabies?*

I can't take my eyes off of the happy family as they leave with their new dogs, with Micah holding Davey's leash, who appears to waggingly approve of his new siblings as he can't stop sniffing them. It is a beautiful sight to see, this newlywed couple starting their life together with a bustling household of cute dogs, riding off into the sunset with their future ahead. I can't wait to do the same with Eli next week, and eventually, find a house with a perfect yard for our dogs. And maybe even add a few more.

Chapter **8**
Let Sleeping Dogs Lie In Bed With You
Samantha

"Hey, Sam. What are you up to today?" Mitchell texts before his shift starts at the pet store, catching me at the perfect time.

I had just processed an approved application for my two darling Chihuahua fosters, and while I am devastated to move them into their "furever" home, I know just how loved they are going to be. It really does make it all worth it. It also doesn't hurt that they are in a home that will be heavily photographed and posted on social media, so I can follow their beautiful journeys and not miss out on anything. Carolyn, while I haven't known her for long, is magnetic and caring, and Micah will be a wonderful provider to them.

It took everything I had not to react to their "married" check mark on the application, but I remained professional. Thankfully, Micah addressed it a few moments later.

"You read that right! This is my bride, and we are here for our children."

Micah's laugh was contagious as I congratulated the beaming couple, telling them what a beautiful pair they made. They thanked me and excitedly greeted the Chihuahua's as I handed them over, giving each a kiss goodbye and whispering in their ears to be good for their new parents. I couldn't help the tears that escaped my eyes, but they really were tears of joy.

"I promise we will take good care of them, Samantha. Little Penelope and Jellybean will continue to have all the love in the world, along with Davey. And of course we will send you lots of pictures, and you can visit us anytime you wish."

"Thank you both. I couldn't be happier that you two are going home with the dogs; to think of anyone else taking them, well, Katie's mom was ready to perform background checks. Then I saw Micah's name come through on an application and I felt instant relief!" I wiped the tears from my eyes, knowing an ugly cry might be coming later, but they had their whole lives ahead of them, and this was the perfect fit. I knew the time was coming to an end fast—I had too many dogs. The Pomeranians were bonded in their own little gang; the Chihuahuas needed a permanent forever. And now they have it.

I call Mitchell instead of texting him back. "Hey, my hands are full so I thought I'd call. I just got the Chi's applications settled, so we said our goodbyes. Katie and her mom are here grooming the kitties. What are you up to today?" I put the phone between my ear and shoulder while I juggle a few felines into a waiting area, so one of my helpers can come in and clean their rooms while they get bathed.

"Oh good, I was just going to ask about that."

It is so like Mitchell to think of the dogs first, and sometimes, I feel disappointed in that.

After a pause, he continues, "And, I was thinking of you, so I thought I'd say hello."

My feelings of heightened interest in Mitchell haven't resurfaced since that evening in the ice cream parlor, thanks to the Lord and his miracles, but now I'm not sure what I'm feeling towards Mitchell. I certainly still like him. Okay, I'm still head over heels, but I'm thinking clearly, and thankful for it.

"Well, aren't you sweet?" I can't help but feel like since I've cooled off from my hot and heavy mindset, the relationship isn't as promising. But then I remember I've never had a godly relationship that wasn't focused on one thing, and I relax. "Carolyn and Micah are married, isn't that great? They eloped on their trip to meet his folks. How cute is that?" I am over the moon for them.

"Wow, that's great news! I look forward to congratulating them in person. And Davey, Micah's dog, liked the Chihuahuas?"

"Yes, he was very friendly, lots of sniffing and no barking. I think Davey is part Chihuahua himself. He's always been so social. I'm overjoyed to see he finally has a few siblings."

Mitchell laughs. "Yes, Davey needs some friends. He's such a cute little thing, but goofy as it gets."

As much as I want to keep the conversation going, I hear screams from the grooming area and think it time to check on Katie and her mother.

"Do you want to have brunch tomorrow at that outdoor I? We could bring a few Pomeranians with us." When I say a 'few', I mean all, and Mitchell knows that. Besides, now that I'm down two dogs, it feels manageable to bring them all in the big cart. And it's quite the sight for people to see a wagon full of fluffy joy, and I love taking them places. They are all just so friendly.

"Sure. How about eleven? Meet you there?"

"Yes! That's great. See you then."

"I love you, Samantha. See you then."

Mitchell hangs up the phone, and I feel the familiar butterflies rising in my stomach, but instead of them turning into another feeling that makes me feel out of control, they stay appropriate. I say a prayer of thanks under my breath and am very excited to see him tomorrow.

Chapter 9
Paws For Love
Katie

After Samantha and I finally convince my mother to go to the emergency room for stitches after Big Orange swung his plush paw at her, and she reacted by ducking and ultimately slipping on the wet floor and busting open an elbow on her fall, it freed up a few minutes for me to figure out what to take to Eli's parents for dinner as I scroll on my phone in the waiting room.

I find a recipe for cherry limeade that I can whip up easily, or so it seems, and had just jotted down the ingredients when my mother comes out of the double doors, being pushed in a wheelchair. "Oh no, are you alright?" I jump to my feet, stumbling over my purse strap that had somehow fallen to the floor, causing me to fall to my knees.

My mother stands immediately, "Katie, don't panic. I'm fine. Freddie here was just wheeling me out for dramatic effect, but I didn't think you'd be in hysterics over it."

Freddie, the nurse, comes over and helps me up.

"I'm fine, thank you. Darn purse strap caught my leg is all." But I look down to see it isn't my purse strap, but it is a dog leash. "Where did this come from?" I hold up the green leash to my mother and Freddie, who shrug, when we hear a shrill cry from the reception area.

"Barnabas has escaped!" The woman, working from her concave of glass windows, runs behind the scenes and comes bursting back through the double doors. "I'm sorry, I was supposed to watch him. His father is receiving care and now he's gone!" She starts wailing and running around, so we follow suit and start looking under chairs and in the bathrooms.

"What kind of dog is it, Miss?" I ask sheepishly, not wanting to disturb her freakout, but needing more information.

"It's a big, white dog. I think he's an Akita or Malamute mix. You can't miss him. That's why I'm kicking myself right now!"

I watch as she peers into small spaces, and Freddie looks under potted plants around the lobby. A moment later, Barnabas comes waltzing through the double doors and returns to his spot where his leash had been, as if nothing happened.

"There you are! You made me so worried!" The woman clips his leash back onto the loop on his collar, sits down in the chair, and says she will wait for his owner to return. "His hand was stuck in a pickle jar. How much longer could it really take?"

I drive us home, since my mother's arm is in a sling.

"Really lame that they put this on me, when it's just my elbow." She takes it off, along with its coordinating neck brace. "I think I'll hold on to this one, though. It may come in handy when I'm using the carpool lane."

"The neck brace? How would that help?"

"It's like when you sneak candy into a movie theater, Katie. Certain things are frowned upon, until it's perceived that something is *wrong with you,* and then they turn a blind eye."

We pull into the grocery store parking lot and my mother says she will wait in the car, but I don't need to leave the keys. I remind her about the bank episode where she set off my car alarm and hit her head on the glass doors, sending the bank into lockdown mode thinking they were getting robbed, so she relents and comes inside.   "But I'm pushing the cart."

After a few seconds, I realize there are several things I needed to restock in my fridge and a few pantry staples for my mother to have while Eli and I are away, so we both begin tossing things into the cart. We start with laundry and dish soap, as mine are nearly out. My mother is busy looking at the store circular to see what the weekly specials are.

"Oh, would you look at that price for Luminol?"

We make our way to the snack food aisle, and I tell her to get whatever she thinks she will need for a week at my house with the dogs. She begins by grabbing a bag of cheese puffs while I go to look at the juices at the end of the aisle. When I turn back to her, the cart looks like it has been filled by a ten-year-old. Chips, candy, and fruit snacks are all over the place.

"Are you having a party while I'm away?" I laugh at the sight, knowing she enjoys her junk food.

"No, but if I did, I'd get that hot dogs and gelatin recipe from Judy. Now that sounds like a hoot."

I feel my stomach churn at the thought as I wrangle some of the chip bags out of the way so I can fit in the ingredients for the cherry punch.

"Alright, anything else?" I ask her, and we decide we will refill the freezer with TV dinners, a large lasagna, and a frozen cheesecake.

She then announces she will go to the produce section, where she studies the rinds of oranges with the spectacle around her neck that she'd used on Carolyn's ring. After adding just one orange that is deemed "acceptable" to the cart, we make our way to the register, where they have a big sale happening for soda.

The boxes are stacked higher than my apartment building, which explains the crane parked inside to help customers take a box from the top. Otherwise, it would be a frightening game of Jenga— possibly deadly, too.

"Katie, grab me some of that cola, will you?"

I nod, signaling to the crane operator for the 24-pack.

"No, Katie. The diet kind. I'm trying to watch what I eat."

*****

Once we make it back to my apartment and put everything away, I grab a cloth sack and put the punch ingredients inside. We will be picking up my father before heading to Eli's parents' house shortly, and we have just a few minutes to get changed and freshen up before we need to leave.

My phone ring and buzzes around on the counter until I retrieve it. It is the clinic calling. Dr. Brand had been so reassuring yesterday that I had almost forgotten about the blood results coming in today. I answer the phone, ready to hear the news.

"Good afternoon, Katie. This is Dr. Brand."

My pulse quickens. Everyone knows that it's never good news when the doctor calls you directly.

"We've detected some elevated levels in your blood sample, and I want to see about a time you can come back in soon. Preferably, this month, if you can."

My heart is now beating in both ears, and I can feel its vibration on my tongue.

"Oh, well, I am actually getting married in a few days and then I'm off to Alaska. May I ask what the urgency is?"

"You may have endometriosis, but I would like to do an exam to be sure. How about tomorrow?"

Wait a minute. Endometriosis? That sounds serious. "Give me the time and I'll be there."

Once Dr. Brand is finished scheduling my exam for the next day, I hang up the phone just in time for my mother to come around the corner.

"I like your outfit, Katie."

I look down at my baggy shirt and cat shampoo-stained jeans that I wore to the animal shelter. "You do?" I look at her in confusion. "This is the outfit reserved for cleaning, painting, and mud wrestling... I'm not wearing this; you know that, right?"

My mother puts her hands up, and mentions she is planning on changing once we hit the hotel.

"Okay, okay. Whatever. I was just giving you a compliment."

I laugh as I go to my room and change into an identical pair of jeans that are fresh, a shirt in a different color, and white tennis shoes. I wash up and re-apply makeup, brush out my ponytail, and dropped my engagement ring into some cleaning solution while I brush my teeth. When it is clean, I rinse it off and marvel at its sparkling.

My mind is heavy with the thoughts of my conversation with Dr. Brand, but I don't want to get everyone in a big tizzy tonight, so I say a quiet prayer for peace.

"Dear Jesus,
Keep my heart from worry, Lord.
Calm my mind from fear.

I pray for strength in the unknown.
In your name,
Amen."

Before we leave, I feed Dolly and talk to her for a few minutes. While she has gotten constant attention this week, we haven't had much one-on-one time, and she needs to know that she is still the special princess of my heart. "Dolly, we are going over to Eli's parents' house tonight, and they have bigger doggies that we haven't introduced you to yet, so just to be extra careful, we are going to keep you at home. Okay, sweetie? Mommy will miss you and will be home in just a little while. I'll leave the bird channel on the TV. Would that be fun? And I just washed your bedding, so it will be extra warm and cozy. And maybe tomorrow, we can go for long *walkies* or a trip to the park. Doesn't that sound fun?"

As far as I am concerned, Dolly seems to love everything I say and happily agrees to it. When I get up from where she is eating, my mother is looking at me with a quizzical look.

"What?" I ask her, expecting her to poke fun at something I said, but she doesn't. It is a look of concern.

"Don't make promises you can't keep, Katie. The weather is bad tomorrow, too."

The sound of the rain picking up makes me groan, but remembering how cute my pink rain slicker makes the weather palatable. "We have matching rain gear, remember?"

My mother laughs, nodding her head. "How could I forget? Apparently, you two are irresistible in it. Here I was, thinking matching your dog was a sign of mental illness. There are a lot of things I love about the twenty-first century, and the right to be adorable is one of them."

"Awfully funny you would accuse me of mental illness, but alright."

We both tease each other the entire ride over.

We pick up my father from his hotel and rearrange all my punch making supplies in the trunk of the rental car before driving over to Eli's parents' home. I have a large jug of limeade, two bottles of cherry juice, lemon lime soda, a big bag of ice, and a bowl to mix it all together. All that is missing is a set of diabetic testing strips once consumed.

Eli's parents live on a beautiful, tree-lined street. The homes look slightly different; Some have craftsman style architecture with bright colored doors, while others are small but with Victorian vibes. His parents have a two-story Tudor with a fresh coat of muted gray paint, a meticulously kept front yard, and bright tulips in the flower beds.

"I didn't even know tulips were in season," my father points as soon as we pull up.

My parents are discussing how Eli's parents have the nicest house and yard in the dreamy neighborhood and are wondering out loud what kind of people they are as I jump out and open the trunk of the SUV.

"Okay, guys, look...I know his parents are neat nicks, and our family couldn't be farther from that, but they are nice people, and not uppity. So just be yourselves. Well, maybe not completely yourselves, but like the best version of yourselves. Capiche?"

When they do not *capiche,* I peer into the front seat and see they are fumbling with something.

"What are you rambling on about, Katie? I can't get my camcorder to turn on."

I looked in horror as my mother is trying to film the occasion.

"Oh, there it goes." She clears her throat and steps out of the car. "Here we are at Katie's future in-laws' home. Look at how nice their front yard is. Talk about curb appeal. Or is it simply a front for something more... sinister?"

I jump in front of the camera and put my hand over the lens and plead with my mother to put it away, which she laughingly obliges. It is barely out of sight when I realize Eli's parents have been watching us from the living room the entire time.

Eli pulls up in his car a few seconds later, hopefully creating enough of a diversion that his parents will forget what they just saw. But I could swear his mother was holding a pad and paper, taking notes.

"Hello future wife." Eli runs over to kiss my forehead and grab the stuff out of the trunk. "What did the doctor say?"

He looks deep into my eyes, and I ramble off about telling him later, to which he agrees.

"Here, let's go inside and meet the parents, shall we?"

He is now addressing my parents, who are acting like a fish out of water. They are walking straighter, stiffer, and seem...stuffy? I shrug it off, just relieved the camcorder is nowhere in sight. My mother is carrying an unusually large bag, but that's beside the point.

Eli's parents open the door for us and say hello to their son and I first before I introduce them to my parents.

"Marsha, Pete, these are my parents."

They shake hands cordially, my parents saying little in return but smiling quite a bit, and I'm thinking they took my speech earlier to heart, when my mother whips out her phone, complete with a stylus, for them to sign her consent form to a background check. I start laughing loudly and walk over to my mother, taking it out of her hand.

"You are such a riot, mom."

They, too, start laughing and share about how Eli's sister Audrey said my mother offered her the same thing. "I've heard your 'shtick' is the true crime thing. Absolutely hilarious."

Pete and Marsha laugh their way into the dining room, where they lead everyone, and Eli and I go to the kitchen to assemble my punch.

"Why, I feel like I already know you, since we've been friends online since the kids started dating."

Marsha and my mother continue their conversation as I turn to Eli.

When we are by ourselves, I look at him to see if he thinks my parents are crazy. He just smiles at me every time I look his way, and once, he winked. It always makes me blush because he is just so masculine and handsome to me. But finally, I flat out ask. "Do you think my mother is... weird? Crazy? *Mentally ill?*"

Eli lets out a roar of laughter and shakes his head, slightly nodding at the end. "About that, Katie. I think she's hilarious. Is she a little... Goofy? Of course she is. Whatever she is, or isn't, she's the good kind of it. And I find her very entertaining."

I thank him for making me feel like any of this is normal, and he smiles. "You never have to worry about that with me, Katie. I think she's a blast, and you and your fun family are just what mine needs."

Eli carries out the nearly overflowing punch bowl to a hutch in the dining room that has a large ladle and glasses, along with a stack of white cocktail napkins. I am elated to see Eli's parents are laughing uncontrollably at a story retelling from my father. "I never considered the insurance adjuster wouldn't know I was joking when

I said the back shed was our family side hustle—*a meth lab.* Boy, did our rates go up!"

Once the laughter subsides, Eli's mom quips, "And how did that make you feel?"

Pete looks over at her with a smirk and shrugs. It is then that I realize, while my mother can't turn off her sleuthing, and my dad his weird jokes, Eli's mother can't turn off her psychological analysis. Eli smiles at me, as he knows I notice it, and I feel better about everything.

After everyone downs some of my overly sweet punch, Pete stands to retrieve the appetizers out of the kitchen when my father offers to help him. Eli and I are engrossed in the conversation our mothers are having, and both of us look at each other in disbelief that they are hitting it off so well. Not that we didn't think they would like each other, as they have been conversing casually over social media since we got together, but they are gabbing on like old friends when they discover they have shared interests.

As our fathers return to the table, each with a cheese and fruit platter in hand, their heated discussion about racquetball supersedes anything else, and we all tune in.

"That's why I always recommend my partner wear a helmet—with my limited spatial awareness caused by partial blindness in my right eye and complete deafness in my left ear—I've been told watching me is a *racket.*" My father smiles at his own joke. "But Pete, I'd love for you to join. There's a club right by my hotel, in fact."

"Oh, we can definitely do that. There's nothing I'd rather do. Say, what shoes are you wearing? The rain has stopped and there's a court two blocks away. I have extra—".

Pete was cut off by Marsha who reminded him we are about to eat dinner.

"But I don't wanna!" Pete pleaded, as my father looked at my mother with wide eyes.

"We just want to go outside and play. We aren't hungry."

My mother shrugs and said she doesn't mind if it is okay with Eli's mother, who also relents.

"Be back before the streetlights come on, and not a moment later. We have fun wedding things to discuss with the happy couple."

Eli and I watch as Marsha gives the orders to our fathers who are out of the room instantly. We hear their excited chatter until they make it to the street.

My mother and Marsha can't interrupt their gabbing for dinner, each barely touching the colorful pasta that Marsha has prepared and only taking a small bite when the other is talking. Then, they each excitedly wait to jump back into talking with whatever they think is relevant to the topic. Eli and I finish our plates and have a second serving of homemade garlic bread.

"I hope you'll be bringing this recipe into our marriage."

I wink at Eli as I take my last bite of the perfectly crisp bread. "Oh yes, of course I will. Along with many, many others. My late grandmother was Italian, and we have quite the arsenal of good recipes. Just you wait."

He pats my hand as we get up and start collecting the dishes from the table, just as our fathers return from their quick game of racquetball.

"Do you feel like dessert?" Eli asks as he lifts a cake plate from the refrigerator. It is a beautiful, buttercream frosted cake, artfully topped with strawberries.

"Do you even know me?" I quip back, nodding in agreement.

We cut slices out of the beautiful creation and place four generous servings on dessert plates with small forks and carry them into the living room, with Eli balancing four on his hands.

"I worked a summer at the Olive Pit in high school." He laughs as I marvel at his plate carrying capabilities.

"You never told me that! Do you have any of their trade secrets?"

"I can recreate the salad, and that's about it."

"The infamous Italian salad with enough red onions to give you breath *that could kill* for a month. I'm the luckiest girl in the world!"

"Did someone say, bread that could kill? Because I have experience with that case," my mother pipes up.

We all laugh, and I shake my head as we dive into the beautiful cake.

Chapter 10
Home Is Where The Dogs Are
Carolyn

Married life has been grand. I moved into Micah's bungalow on the outskirts of town, which he bought a year ago and has been fixing up. There's a fenced backyard, two little plots for garden beds and a rickety front porch. He's finished working on the inside, meaning there's no longer any nails laying around or rotten windows, which I can't imagine living in, but he said it's been a blast to put sweat equity into a home. I'm thoroughly impressed by his handy ability, and with my decorating, this house really does feel like a home.

Is it our home, though? Micah has heard nothing but my ideas about leaving here for Wyoming since we got home from our whirlwind engagement and marriage trip. His main reason for leaving there was college, but now he's unsure about the job opportunities.

"I want to be a provider to my family."

He has said that many times over, and I love him for it, but I am feeling differently.

"Thank you for that, Micah. Right now, it's just you, me, and these three little fur babies. We can go anywhere we want in the world. We can figure it out together. If we wait until there are more of us, I don't know how easy it will be. Do you see us staying here, in this house forever?"

The house is amazing, and after seeing its before pictures and knowing what went into it, Micah could have success anywhere. But to me, success is not just financial. It's happiness. It's family.

"I have always pictured myself fixing it up and either renting it out to a family or selling it. Like a flip. I enjoy my department here, but I can fight fire anywhere. Honestly, I am surprised you liked Wyoming that much. I took you as more of a city girl, but it would be wonderful to go back."

Hearing him say these words makes everything in my life align.

It is settled then. We will be moving to Wyoming. For me, it is going to be a fresh start, not that I need one, but I have been craving a new place that I can begin my married life in. We discuss our plans for work, and I think it is important for me to find a job right off the bat so I can start meeting people and getting to know my new community, but I want a fun job —something that doesn't keep me up at night with stress or drama. He reminds me of the coffee shops and a retail store that I could apply to, and I am looking forward to the prospect. Micah will start out by helping his parents on the ranch.

"We could live in one of the ranch hand cabins, to start. But not sure what the dogs would think of all that mooing going on?" He starts cackling uncontrollably.

Micah's family has several hundred cattle that they work, but from the sounds of it, they spread them out over several different land leases to graze, so they are not often on the ranch. Meanwhile, they raise and train horses for auctions.

Micah calls his parents and runs the idea past them. "Hey, mom, dad. Yeah, she sure is." Micah winks at me, as he has his parents on speakerphone, and they ask if I am still missing them. "That's why I'm calling. What would you say if we moved home? Carolyn wants to start our lives together closer to family and she just loves Wyoming."

To say they are over the moon is an understatement. I don't know how long the cheering goes on, but I know Micah has to turn the volume down on his phone. One of the dogs' barks at the mail being delivered, so I run into the other room to pick up the envelopes from the slot.

When I come back in, I hear the best news.

"And you and Carolyn can live in one of the ranch cabins. You know this is your home—you can stay in one for the rest of your lives if that's what you wish. I'll get the two-bedroom cabin ready for your homecoming!"

I am overjoyed. Not only do we get a fresh start, with family, but a soft landing with a darling little cabin to live in. Micah promises to keep them in the loop with updates and ends the call after a few more minutes.

Picking up our three darling doggies and cuddling together as a family on the couch, we make our plans for the future.

"Really, the porch could fly with just a coat of paint. It's squeaky, but it's up to code."

I can tell Micah is starting to get the zoomies as he thinks about it.

"Heck, we can be on our way after putting a sign in the yard, if you want!"

As much as I want to say yes to that, I know there are a few loose ends we need to tie up first, such as, we need to paint that front porch. I can help out our curb appeal by planting some flowers in the front and setting out some cute furniture on the porch. I'd only unpacked my clothing and necessities as we've been so busy since I moved in, so that is a bonus, as we can just throw it all on a truck again when we leave. Of course, I'll need to give notice to my job, but that is a breeze. Micah says if we are serious about the move, I should just put my notice in now, that way, we have more time to prepare the house for selling, so I plan a short resignation letter in my head. It is all coming together perfectly.

There is just one other thing: We have a wedding to attend.

Chapter 11
Tail Spins
Katie

"Well, I don't think that could have gone any better," I told Eli as we share the chore of doing the dishes from the evening while our parents sit in the living room.

Pete is animatedly reenacting my father's serve while they critique each other, but both are impressed with the other's game. And it turns out, Marsha has done a little reading on the Kyle Hamburg case, which opens a can of worms that pleases both women to no end as there is nothing either of them love discussing more than the criminal mind.

"I told you, Katie. I knew this would happen tonight. You'd only met my parents a few times before, and we hadn't spent much time together with them, so I thought I'd keep it as a surprise," Eli grinned.

"A surprise? That your parents are also weird?"

We both laugh and Eli, drying the last plate and putting it away, says, "Yes," and then, Katie, there are so many reasons why you are my perfect person." He puts his hands on my shoulders like we are about to sway at the school dance, with two Bibles between us. "Now, do you want to tell me what the doctor said?"

Fear strikes my heart once more as I melt into his arms and let him hold me, with tears escaping my eyes and falling onto his shirt. I desperately want to hug him back, so I wrap my arms around him. I tell him about the possibility of me having endometriosis.

"Whatever happens, Katie, we will work through it. There's nothing we can't face together through prayer. God will show us the way."

Eli laughs as my soapy hands are around his neck. I grin, and he wipes away my tears, and we return to our parents.

"Speaking of Audrey," Marsha chimes in, "we've gotten a call that Audrey and her fiancé, Jeff, are changing their wedding plans."

I let out an audible gasp, as at first, I think that means the wedding is off.

"Don't worry, they are still getting married. My guess is, they are going to elope, because that mother of his. . . It's a real shame, is all. But that's just my guess, none of my business."

Marsha puts her hands in the air, and I catch a twinkle in my mother's eye and know that she has much to say about Audrey's future mother-in-law, but for once, biting her tongue.

As we gather up our shoes and sweaters to leave, our mothers are making plans to keep in touch before the wedding, and our fathers already have time reserved for the racquetball courts the following day.

"I think this was a big hit," Eli says as he walks me to the car. "Imagine our holiday gatherings!" We both chuckle at the thought of our goofy parents when adding in a little Christmas cheer. "We have so much to look forward to, Katie Skatey." He smiles ear to ear; the rhyming of my soon-to-be name still makes us both laugh.

"I wouldn't want to do this with anyone else." I say, as he kisses my forehead while my parents get into the front seat of the car, still waving off Marsha and Pete.

My parents excitedly speak about their new best friends the entire way home; not in a conversation with each other, but rather, obliviously both talking to me at the same time. Somehow, I tune it all out, feeling blessed and thankful for them and Eli's parents and how wonderful everything has gone. My mother decides she will stay with my father at the hotel for the remainder of time until the wedding, considering I have just a few days left to live alone. I am happy with the idea that I will be able to sleep in and not have to worry about a house guest, but also that it gives me more days for Dolly to be the only furbaby in my life.

When they drop me off at my apartment, I tell them both goodnight and run up my stairs and go inside to greet Dolly. I cannot wait to tell her about the evening. It is only 8 p.m., and we have time to watch a movie without me falling asleep halfway through, which elates me as that is our nightly routine, but will soon be changing.

I get into cozy pajamas and scoop Dolly up as we go for the couch. Her brush is sitting on the coffee table, so I slowly run it through her precious little curls, giving her head a massage. She is putty in my arms after just a few swipes. I look at her with overwhelming love and turn on the movie.

*****

The next morning is my wedding dress fitting at the bridal shop. My mother calls around ten to see if I want to go grab breakfast with her and my father beforehand, which I agree to. She gets us a table at the "Blitz & Bones" doggy cafe, and Dolly is dressed and ready by the time they arrive to pick me up.
The moment we walk in, Edward starts whining.

"What is it, mom? Does he sense someone has an exposed artery in the general vicinity?"

"I'm not sure, let's see what he wants." She unzips the front of his stroller, and I imagine him lunging out, snarling teeth at the nearest stranger, but instead, he has the look of love on his face. We all follow the direction of his stare, and I laugh when I see it is directed at Liam, the owner of the cafe, who is wearing a dog collar and passing out treats to his four-legged customers. He makes eyes with Edward, who is now wagging with his entire body as Liam walks over with the dog bowl of bones.

"Well, hello, sir. And what is your name?"

"That's Edward," I look in awe, waiting for any minute little Eddie to snap and bite him. But he doesn't.

"May he have a treat? They are egg, dairy, gluten, and soy free."

My dad laughs, mouthing, "What's left?" as my mother obliges.

"Oh yes! Edward would love that. Thank you so much!"

Edward politely takes the treat from his hand and leaves Liam with all five fingers intact. I am so impressed that I reach over to pet his head and am immediately met with a deep guttural growl that is so frightening, I could lose bladder control.

After ordering omelets, hashbrowns, and three cups of "Bark Roast Coffee," we eat our meal and Dolly and Edward each top off their bones with a Puppachino, which is just a cup of whipped cream.

"Dogs have it so easy," my father grunts with laughter, watching them lap up the Puppachino. "Who else can wildly eat whipped cream with no abandon out in public, and strangers will find it endearing? If I did that, there's a chance the cops would be called on me."

I clink coffee cups with him in agreement while my mother pays the bill. "We better get going, Katie. Don't want to be late for your dress fitting appointment. And I must get Edward dropped off at his grooming appointment at PetWorld beforehand. He wants a specific fade."

As we drop off Edward for his grooming appointment, I take Dolly inside to say hello to Mitchell. He has been excited to see Dolly and says that Eli had just been in a few days ago for Carter's grooming appointment. We speak for a few minutes before a line forms at the checkout, and he has to go.

"Samantha and I will see you at the wedding! Of course, since she will be a bridesmaid, I am going to be watching from the pews. Can't wait!"

We say our goodbyes and as I push Dolly down the aisles in her stroller, it sinks in that the next time I will be here, I will be changing her last name on her grooming profile to match her new dad and brother. There is something so cute about the prospect, and then I remember we might be moving from here soon. What will my life look like in a month's time? Six months? A year? So many unknowns circle around in my head. But then I remember all my days are written out in the book of life. God knows every hair on my head and what my life will bring. I've met several people since I moved here years ago, but most came after I adopted Dolly. That was such an unexpected blessing in my life that's helped me grow in my faith and fellowship. I will miss them all if we move away, but I can't help but feel excited for the prospect of a new adventure.

"Dear Jesus,

I trust the plan You have for my life, whatever that may be.

I pray for Your continued peace and contentment to unfold in every situation that I find myself in.

In your name,

Amen."

When we arrive at *The Hitching Post*, I am surprised to see two other brides getting fitted for their dresses at the same time as my appointment. It is Raquel working today, and now I see why Rachel said people mix them up. They are positively identical, down to the haircuts. They even dress similarly, and Raquel's handwriting on her nametag catches me off guard. The "qu" somehow looks like a swirly "ch," and I distinctly remember Rachel's nametag having bold, widely spaced letters. Now I know why.

As I come out of the fitting room, Raquel follows, as she helps me into the dress and makes sure I can get on the pedestal without tripping on the dress. Once I am on, relishing the perfect fit of the gown, she retrieves the veil and places it into my hair. It is beautiful. I turn to see my parents who are overjoyed at the fit.

"You couldn't look any more beautiful, Katie."

The other brides in the room turn and agree with their words, both overjoyed for me as I for them. We chat with the women and are suddenly in a circle sharing about our future husbands.

The woman on my right introduces herself as Harper. She is to marry her college sweetheart, Clay, at their church in two weeks. They are going to immediately move to his hometown of Charlotte, North Carolina after the big day when he will join his father's construction equipment sales company. Harper tells us about her singing career and how she is excited to join his family's church because they have reserved an opening in the choir just for her.

Both ladies look to me next, where I share about our church wedding at the Three Maples this weekend, and our Alaskan honeymoon. When asked how we met, I share that I was hit in the head with a miniature frisbee at the Bark Park, after adopting a dog we'd later surmised was his dog's sibling. The whole shop is giggling and clapping at the coincidence and wishes us a lifetime of happiness. Then I take the lead and ask the woman to my left, Evelyn, about her wedding day.

Evelyn smiles and speaks about how they met at a basketball game, and it was each of their second marriages. She stops talking after that, assuming the conversation has ended, until Harper asks where the wedding is being held.

"We are getting married in our backyard by my oldest brother. It's just going to be us and some family, nothing special."

Evelyn has a sadness about her, but I can't quite put my finger on what. The dress she is wearing is stunning; it is a silky, drop neck spaghetti strap dress that goes all the way to the floor. It isn't overly fitted but still reveals a lovely figure. She has paired it with timeless jewelry and matching shoes that are all in its eggshell white color.

"You look amazing, Evelyn. I hope you'll get lots of pictures—that is a dress to remember!" I don't really know what to say, as there seems to be something touchy going on, so I speak from the heart.

As Harper goes back to her dressing room to change back into her clothes, Evelyn does the same, and I realize that she is there alone, while Harper and I have family in attendance.

Raquel comes over to me and puts the belt on with the delicate purple flowers. "Is there anything else you think the dress needs? Or are you satisfied with it?"

The dress is flawless. I have enough room to breathe, eat cake, and maybe even dance, the thought of which makes my hands instantly sweaty, yet the dress makes me look quite fit. "It's perfect, Raquel. I can't wait to wear it!"

She happily leads me to the fitting room where she helps unbutton, unzip, untie, unclamp, and unscrew all the things that hold a wedding dress together. Once she leaves, I change back into my clothes and meet my parents at the front, where she has the dress in a protective plastic forcefield with a brown dress bag over it, so no one can see inside.

My father takes the dress, saying he is going to lay it in the back of the car while we finish things up inside. I pull out my wallet to pay for the dress, but my mother waves me off.

"Katie, let us get this for you. You wouldn't let us cover the wedding costs, so we'd like to get your dress."

I thank her profusely and tell her what a tremendous help that is. It is true; we hadn't asked our parents for help paying for our wedding. Instead, we chose to keep it small; the most expensive cost is our cake, but it turns out that the owner of the Pup Street Bakery has a sister who makes wedding cakes on the side, while utilizing the commercial kitchen at Pup Street. While it is still expensive, it is hundreds less than what it would have cost from a larger bakery.

While my mother is chatting up Raquel about the post-wedding dress preserving details, Evelyn walks out to leave.

"Hey, it was nice chatting with you today." I say, meeting her eyes after a moment. While she doesn't look like she's been crying, she may be close to tears.

"Oh, thank you, I enjoyed talking to you as well. Good luck at your wedding," she casually speaks, looking towards the door.

I look in that direction and see my father hanging up my dress on the hook inside the car. I feel so very blessed to have them here with me today, and it reminds me that Evelyn has been alone.

"When is your wedding?" I ask her.

"In a week from today." She smiles, but it doesn't reach her eyes. "Am I doing the right thing?"

I am taken back by her question and tell her I'll walk her to her car.

"What do you mean, Evelyn?"

"My first marriage was so hard. We had every problem imaginable, and it didn't end well. And then, after a long and messy divorce, I met Trey, and nothing could be easier. But I can't help but feel I don't deserve it, and that God's grace won't cover me. I know people say He will forgive me, but I just don't see how."

"I totally understand how you are feeling, Evelyn. I've made some unbelievable mistakes in my life that have caused me to lie awake at night and wonder if I can be forgiven. But the Bible makes it clear: You will be forgiven for your sins if you ask for it and forgive others for their sins against you. His grace *is* real, and He provides all the peace and healing you may require. You do deserve love, and above all, Jesus is waiting for you to take the free gift of His."

Evelyn nods, taking it in. "And then there's Trey. He says he's been waiting his whole life to meet me and that I'm an answer to his prayers, but I feel like damaged goods."

"Embrace grace, Evelyn. Jesus meant it when He died for all of our sins, not just some of them. You can trust that His grace is more than sufficient."

Katies Biblical Application

I made a new friend in Evelyn, and before she left, I invited her to Eli's Bark Park Ministry. Evelyn laughed, saying that she had two greyhounds that would love to come. She pulled out her phone, and the lock screen picture was two beautiful, athletic-looking dogs in matching turtleneck sweaters.

"They love to dress up," she giggled, pulling up a few more pictures of them in rain gear, Christmas pajamas, and then a photo of them as Leprechauns. "That's Trey," Evelyn pointed to a bearded, burly man that was dressed up as a pot of gold next to the dogs. We were both laughing hysterically at the pictures.

"He seems like a good sport!" I laughed, and she interjected.

"This is all him, I promise. The only thing they owned when I met Trey was those turtleneck sweaters. I knew I was in for it when a week after we met, he got a PetWorld credit card. He sure does love those dogs, and thankfully, they love him back!"

I agreed with her, and we talked about how hard it would be if our dogs didn't like our future husbands.

"I know for me; I wouldn't date them anymore. If my dog doesn't like you, how could I?"

We laughed for a few more minutes when my mother emerged from the shop. I hugged Evelyn goodbye and gave her my phone number.

*****

When we pick up Edward from his grooming appointment, he is unusually calm and collected. As we walk up to the windows, I had pictured him wearing a muzzle and straight jacket so they could file his nails or clean his ears. But instead, we walk up to a completely normal scene where he is looking at the groomer lovingly.

"What the heck?" I ask rhetorically, but my mother knows *exactly* what I am referring to.

"Whenever there is just one woman present, and no men, Edward feels safe enough to love. It's really kind of sad when you think about it."

It is sad. I know I have misjudged that little guy, but every chance I've given him, he's tried to rip me apart. Looking at him now, from a safe distance and 3 inches of plexiglass between us like we are visiting him in prison, I can admire his darling haircut, a little black bow tie around his neck, and the clear coat of "pawlish" on his nails. Wait a minute.

"Did they file his nails into points?" my mother laughs and walks into the grooming area, dismissing my question as I look on in horror.

*****

The next stop is my follow-up with Dr. Brand. My earlier nerves have been replaced with the peace from the Holy Spirit, so when my mother drops me off outside of the clinic, I bravely waltz inside. After a nearly silent exam from the doctor, I don't know what to expect. She excuses herself and announces she will return in a few minutes. As I sit in the paper gown, pondering why something so stressful is paired with a getup that equally brings anxiety, Dr. Brand enters the room.

"Thank you for your patience, Katie. With our exams, I have confirmed you have a case of endometriosis. It's not uncommon that such a thing disrupts your blood sugar levels, leading to dizziness, but I'm not ruling out hormonal imbalances, either. I'd like to do some more testing once you are home from your honeymoon. But for now, I'd like to answer any questions you may have."

I am at a loss for words. I haven't yet done so much as an internet search for this condition, let alone drafted a list of questions. "What does this mean for me?"

"It could mean you need to be placed on a dose of estrogen to combat symptoms. You may need pain relievers from time to time. Unfortunately, you may also struggle with infertility."

My heart drops to the floor. "Infertility?" I questioned her diagnosis, as if doing so may reverse course. "But I'm getting married, and—".

Dr. Brand cuts me off. "I know, Katie. And I'm so sorry. But don't give up hope, okay? There are lots of things we can try, if or when you cross that bridge. It's not for sure you will have these struggles."

I leave the appointment feeling lost. Do I want children? Well, I don't know. But to have something potentially decided for me feels rough and unsettling. What if I do want them down the road? What if Eli decides he wants children, and I can't? What if... My mind is racing with all the possibilities. There is only one thing I can do: drive to Eli's and tell him. As much as I love him, he has to know that I may never be able to have children, and I shake with the realization this could end us.

As if my inner emotions are affecting the weather, heavy raindrops start pouring from the sky. I pray the entire drive over, and when I arrive, I feel better than I had at the clinic.

Eli answers quickly after I knock; his eyes filled with surprise. "Katie! I wasn't expecting you. Is everything okay?"

I walk in and sit on his couch. "No. It's not." Tears well in my eyes again as I tell him the news. "I may never be able to have children... And I understand if you want to call things off." I peek up at Eli, whose eyes are wider than the man who discovered that parrots could talk.

"Katie, I—I'm speechless."

My heart sinks to my stomach as my worst fears are coming true. This is a dealbreaker for him.

But then he continues. "I am sad that you would think there is any diagnosis that could make me stop loving you."

"Are you sure? What if I can't have children?"

"Truthfully, if we wanted children one day, and we couldn't conceive, I don't see why we couldn't adopt. Just like Dolly and Carter—does adopting make them any less ours? To me, it doesn't."

I laugh through my tears as he compares our fur babies to our future hypothetical human babies. "You're right; I feel the same way. I was just worried because we hadn't really decided about having children to begin with, and then I get this news."

"You becoming my wife means so much more to me than this. I promise you; we will figure it out. God has a greater plan for us. So, tell me, will you need any treatments for endometriosis?"

We spend another hour talking as we sit on his couch, his arm wrapped around me tightly. Eli makes it clear he isn't afraid of life when it gets messy, and I am thankful for it. As the afternoon is winding down, I get up to leave, but not before asking another question.

"You know when you said there was no diagnosis that could make you stop loving me? What about monkeypox? Or mad cow disease?"

He kisses my forehead and laughs. "Even that weird disease that makes your skin glow in the dark. In fact, that might be really convenient while camping."

He motions for me to wait. "I'm just about done here; I'll walk you out."

Eli quickly finishes getting ready for his parents' house, where he will be for the next two nights up until the wedding, where the young men from the youth group he leads are coming for a dinner party, potluck style, and fellowship. As he grabs his bags, he tells me about their plans.

"It sounds like fun."

"Getting through the next two days will be hard; I can't wait to be your husband."

"You're almost there."

"I love you Katie... Soon-to-be Skatey."

"I love you too, Eli."

*****

The next morning, my mother hands me a spray tan information guide. It outlines the things to do and not to do, before and the following four hours after a spray tan.

"Allegedly," she starts, "we are to exfoliate heavily beforehand. But that contradicts what I read online."

Oh no, I think.

Katie's Words of Law
Burden of Proof
Noun
The duty of proving whatever you read online to be false.

"I think I will go by the brochure. I'm just getting a light mist anyway; it says here there are *levels* of color."

"Like how there are levels to mental illness, Katie. Look— do what you feel is right, but I am not going to be happy if I'm the color of a papaya in our wedding photos."

"I don't like how you said *our.*"

"Oh stop, you know what I mean."

"Do I, though?" A knock on the door interrupts us.

"That must be Marge."

I look in amazement as my mother answers the door, and it is Marge.

"Good morning! Come on in. Can I get you anything?"

"Is that coffee?" Marge asks my mother as she points to my pot brewing on the counter.

"Yes. Cream or sugar?"

Marge smiles. "Both! Thanks."

I've yet to address or be addressed, so I interject. "Hi, Marge. What's up?"

"Your mother and I are working on a little something together."

Suddenly an image of the two of them on Dateline *Wedding Edition* pops into my head.

"Is that so?" I turn to look at my mother who is dragging out the coffee making process so she won't have to make eye contact with me.

"Mom?" I prompt her to turn around, as she would never want to appear rude in front of a guest.

"Okay, pull it out of me, why don't you? I have a surprise for you and Eli is all. Marge is going to have Patricia take professional photos of Carter and Dolly while I'm here pet sitting."

My heart explodes when I hear the news. "Really? Oh, my word, THANK YOU!" I jump up, hugging her.

She is so pleased at the news that I love it. "

That's so perfect. Ugh, sorry I was bratty about it. I'll let it be a complete surprise to Eli; he's going to love it so much too."

"Well, I'm glad. It's my gift to the couple."

We hug again and then while embracing, Marge comes over and hugs us both.

Marge speaks. "Patricia is out on location this week for *Doggy Vogue.* They are shooting all over Des Moine, Iowa. Advertising a new fashion line for the working pup. Blazers, pencil skirts, sock suspenders like they did in the old days—you name it."

My mind goes blank. I hadn't considered Marge for taking pictures of my creations before and decide I could look into that someday.

"Wow, she's really made the big time! But I knew she would get the gig once she submitted those sample pictures from her studio. She wasn't sure about the bulldog car mechanic setup, but I managed to convince her." My mother smiles, eagerly accepting praise from Marge.

"Agreed. I'm so glad you encouraged her, as she wouldn't listen to me. Said I'm biased because I help her design her sets. Anyway, she'll be back soon, and I can't wait to see what she does with the poodles."

My mother and Marge get down to business with a few backdrop selections, holding up Dolly to each one before finally settling on the one that "brings out her eyes." Since they are *twin* dogs, and as my mother always argues there is no such thing, they are confident the color selection is perfect, and Marge leaves with a promise she'll be back after the wedding, with Patricia and her complete setup.

After thanking my mother repeatedly, we discuss where the pictures could go and then I take to the shower, gently exfoliating as the brochure recommends. We both hurry to get ready for our appointments and decide we'll take the brochure's advice on wearing very loose clothing.

"Now, I wish I had something that made it look like I was wearing a diaper, too. All I have are these baggy sweatpants, but the band around my ankle might rub on my tan."

We load Dolly into the car. Since I will be away from her for a week, I want to spend as much time with her as I can. Once we are all securely strapped in, we head towards the tanning place.

Chapter 12
It's A Ruff Life
Samantha

I never considered having children. In the past, the idea of having a child scared me out of my wits. But now? Not out of wedlock of course. But now, as I am having lunch at the park, the dogs are off with Mitchell who's throwing miniature frisbees at them, and I can't unglue my eyes from the children playing with their dogs. One mom has her baby in a carrier while she watches her doodle running laps around a husky. Another woman, pregnant, sitting on the bench. I can't tell which dog is hers.

Surely, there have always been children, moms, and pregnant women here. But why am I just now noticing them? Why does it feel like it's all I can see, everywhere I go? Why can I not stop thinking about being a mother?

My internal battle with feelings of lust has passed me. I can thank God for that. But it almost feels it was replaced with another desire. Of motherhood. I truthfully don't know how Mitchell feels about such things, and I know I need to bring it up, *stat*.

As if on cue, Mitchell comes back to finish his sandwich, a handful of Pomeranians trailing him.

"Okay, okay." The dogs are excitedly yapping away as he pulls out a bag of treats. "Sit. Everyone, sit. I'm waiting."

The group is anxious for their snacks but tries their best to be patient. Watching them is heartwarming, and again, I wonder if I am really wanting motherhood, or if this is enough. I certainly have enough mouths to feed. The question comes fast, pressing my heart: Can't I have both?

"Do you want children?" I never said I had tact, and I admit this could be framed better, but time is of the essence. I need to know how my potential husband feels about something suddenly very important to me.

"Not really, I mean, we have so many as it is." The dogs bark again, but Mitchell politely shushes them as he finishes his lunch. "Thanks for the sandwich—I love this cranberry marmalade you paired with the turkey—it's fantastic."

His words deflate me. I know I can make a mean sandwich, but no children? "When you say, 'not really,' what does that mean?" I hate using air quotes, but this feels dire.

"It means, no. I don't. I'm satisfied in life. I have everything I want. I love my job, my condo... I love the dogs and *you*, Samantha. I don't need anything to change in my life. I have never pictured being a parent. I thought you felt the same. Do you?"

I set my sandwich down. It suddenly feels very dry in my mouth. "I don't know. Maybe. Maybe, I'd like to reserve the option just in case. This is all happening so quickly." Just a week ago, I felt like we connected on every point in the world. And now, I'm not so sure.

"I thought you wanted things to happen quickly. Samantha, we were just discussing marriage because—".

I cut him off. I don't need to rehash that right now. "I know. And you know how I told you I've been struggling with those... temptations? Well, it seems like God has replaced that with a new desire. I'm still working it out, but I have this sudden calling for motherhood, and it's stronger than any other feeling I've ever had."

Laying it all out for Mitchell, I let him take it or leave it. He doesn't say anything for what feel is like an eternity. I remember my prayer at the ice cream parlor; if this isn't exactly what God has intended for me, for Him to slam the doors shut. I take a breath, expecting the doors to be slammed in my face at this very instance.

"I think that's beautiful, Samantha."

What? I feel my jaw drop at his words.

He continues. "Your convictions have always inspired me. And this one is no different. I know you've had your battles, and you've come out stronger than I'll ever be. But-"

I brace for impact.

"—I just don't know about this, Sam. I don't feel the same calling for fatherhood. Then again, I've never had a reason to think about it. Could I pray on it for a few days?"

I happily oblige to his request, I feel satisfied by our conversation, and my mind is calmed by the Holy Spirit. We both gather the dogs up as we have work to return to, and we hug by our cars. It is a warm, familiar embrace that just a week ago was all I could think about. Funny how that works.

Dropping my dogs back off at my apartment, I change out the water in their bowls and imagine for a moment what it would be like if I had a baby. I picture myself wearing one of those carriers strapped to my chest while I am at work. I am the manager. What would the board of directors think about that? Somehow, I don't think they would mind. And I know my parents would be over the moon to help me with babysitting, especially since my mother has retired. Last Christmas, they made a joke about needing a few grandkids to help them out around the house, when I playfully offered up some of the Pomeranians. They've never put any pressure on me to have children, and I've been single for quite some time, so it was all in good fun. But it did make me aware that they would welcome the opportunity.

Chapter 13
Paw Prints On My Heart
Katie

The outside of *Basking Buns* is creepy in the way that most strip malls are. They usually contain questionable *parlors* of all kinds. This one is at least a little more upscale, and I decide it is because they have some potted faux trees outside.

My mother pushes Dolly's stroller inside while I hold the door open for her. We are greeted by a beautifully bronzed woman at the desk.

"Good morning, ladies! Welcome to *Basking Buns.* Do you have an appointment?" Dolly perks up in the stroller and the woman coos at her, coming around from behind the desk to pet her. "May I?"

"Yes, she enjoys pets." I smile. "And we have appointments under Fitzgerald."

"Great! Sprays or bakes?"

The image of an uncooked turkey with the word "*bakes*" takes my mind hostage.

"Sprays, please. And uh, mine is for my wedding tomorrow, so I'd like to keep it gentle, if possible." My anxiety goes through the roof when I let myself toss around the fact I'll be getting married *tomorrow.*

"Congratulations! And of course. Here are our levels." She pulls out a color chart and holds it up to my hand. "I'd say you're a level two right now. What level would you like to be? With your fair complexion, I wouldn't recommend anything beyond a four if you want more of a glow."

"I'll take a seven," my mother hollers out without even looking at the chart.

"Are you sure about that, mom? That's like three shades darker than what she recommends for a glow."

"Everyone looks better tan, Katie. I don't think anything past a four is going to be that noticeable. Besides, I didn't exfoliate so it's going to be layered on top of my body lotion if I change my mind."

"Okay. I guess I'll try a four," I stammer out.

"Perfect. That will give you a sun kissed *glow,* without the bronze sparkles. Does that sound okay?"

That's a relief to hear. "Yes, I definitely do not want sparkles. Thank you."

The woman at the desk finishes typing something up on the computer and assigns me to a room. "Katie, your tan will be ready in room one, right over here to the left."

I look over to my mother and Dolly.

"I'll stay out here with the princess until you're done, then I'll take my turn."

I go into the room and get the spray tan. When it is done, I feel the color is very faint, though the brochure says it will develop more over the next few hours. I am thrilled at how soft it looks.

"Oh Katie, you're glowing!" I tell myself, smiling as I waltz out of the small room, realizing the front desk has a black light turned on in the hallway, and I am wearing light colors. "I think the color is perfect." I sit down on the bench, taking Dolly from her arms.

"Actually, I agree. Miss, can I change to a four?"

"Of course! I'll put you in room one then as well. It's ready when you are."

We finish up our tans and decide to grab a light lunch. We pull into one of those soup and salad buffets that also have all kinds of treats like sweets and bread, and even though it looks like a light meal, you leave so full that you consider calling an ambulance. They have outdoor seating, so we take turns going through the line while the other sits with Dolly. My wedding dress fits great, and while I'm not too concerned about gaining five pounds magically overnight, I decided that I want to eat a little lighter than usual, considering I will be getting photos taken tomorrow, I don't want my face to swell up like it usually does after a big consumption of salt. So, I stick with a few variations of salads they have, and my mother does the same.

"I was thinking we should have some of the girls come over tonight. What do you think?" my mother asks, excitedly.

"That would be so fun—great idea! I'll send a group text out and call Judy."

After a few minutes, everyone confirms.

On the way home, we decide to pick up a few DVDs from the movie rental kiosk outside of the drugstore, for *nostalgia's sake.* This is the biggest bummer to me about the new day and age where everything can be streamed: I miss walking into a video store on a Friday night—the exorbitant late fees, the overpriced candy, and the sheer panic when you've gone in for a specific flick and find nothing behind the box—*it is thrilling.*

Movie rental stores, once a staple of our society, have now been wiped from the earth, only to be replaced by dollar stores, self-serve frozen yogurt places, and chiropractic offices. Growing up, I often wondered what it would be like to work at the rental store. It seemed like most of the job was rewinding tapes in the machine which had only that function to perform. Would there be joy in charging sixty-seven dollars when a busy mom forgot to return a

VHS for three days? Would requiring a credit check to borrow a tape that costs less than ten dollars make you feel empowered? I sure thought so. I couldn't wait to apply when I turned sixteen but imagine my disappointment when they weren't hiring.

"We have a stack of applications this high," the manager grabs three VHS tapes to show me the size. "This is a very desirable place of employment."

Hmm, I wonder why as I look around. Sure, they have a convenient location next to a shopping center. The Krispy Kreme next door is also a plus; if you work here, you could strategically take your breaks whenever the *"Hot n' Fresh"* light is on. But what makes this place that popular, really?

"I'd say, nostalgia." The manager says, adding my application to the stack.

"What?"

"You just asked me what made this place so popular."

Gee, I hadn't realized I said that out loud.

"We can all agree our good childhood memories involved a video store. Look—I can understand your passion for the rental video market. We have a pretty high turnover, but every once in a while, we get a long-term employee, like me. I've worked here for twelve years, Katie. So, if everyone I call over the next few years works about three months on average, I'd say your turn is coming up around 2010. Hang in there, kiddo. You'll get to live the dream one day."

I never did get that call, but by that year, most of those stores were closing, if they hadn't already shuttered their doors for good. I saw the manager years later working as an expo at Chili's.

As our tans start to develop, I am relieved to see mine isn't very noticeable but rather natural. My mother's tan goes the opposite direction, and suddenly, she is looking like a tomato.

"What's going on with your tan?" I turn my head back to the DVD player, hooking up the seven cords for my television to transmit.

"What about it, Katie?"

I look back in disbelief as she's even darker than she was a moment ago. And suspiciously *sparkling.* "What happened to level *four?"* I demand, knowing she pulled some bait and switch at the last minute.

"I didn't want you to worry about the pictures. Most of this will wear off when I shower. I wanted to be left with *some* color, that's all."

"SOME? You're a *burnt orange!"* I reach for the brochure, again comparing the levels of color. "Oh, my word... You're a level eleven, and it only goes to ten." I feel as if I might faint.

"Don't worry about it. Here, how about I shower right now to prove it? Where's that illegal scrub?"

"It's on the counter... and thank you."

"You're welcome. I worry about our photos, too, after all. I have several planned with the five of us."

"Five? Let's see, do you mean you and dad, me and Eli, and.. who else?"

She shakes her head. "No, I mean you, Eli, Carter, Dolly and myself."

All I can do is look at her and laugh while she takes off for the shower.

'   *"Hello, this is Rhonda Meyers reporting from KA4U News. We're back here at the Brooklane Apartment Complex as a woman has reportedly gone missing. I'm standing here with Katie Fitzgerald who tells us that her mother has left abruptly but left behind this suspicious note. Katie, will you read it to us?"*

"Uhm, sure. 'Dear Katie, My spray tan did not come off in the shower like I had hoped. I left to find the colony of orange people in the mountains, but rest assured, I will be back tomorrow to watch the dogs. Don't look for me. And especially don't unlock the bathroom door—I am not in here scrubbing my life away, trying to remove this stain that's taken over my skin.'" I fold the note back up into its origami frog and look back to Rhonda.

"Thank you, Katie. On the eve of your wedding, this sounds like quite an emotional feat to be experiencing. I have heard rumors of this orange colony; I even considered it once for myself after a really bad experience in a tanning bed, but they aren't accepting any new residents. It is quite exclusive, I guess.'"

"Oh wait—is that her car in the guest spot?" I point to the one with rental plates.

"Katie, did you not check the bathroom before you called us?" (Runs away)

I hold my breath as I hear the bathroom door open and my mother emerge, and I release it once I see she is back to looking normal. I am pleased that most of the tan did in fact, wash off in the water. I nod at her approvingly and say a silent prayer of thanks. We get ready to watch the movie, each taking our place on the long couch with Dolly.

"I can't believe that tomorrow, I will finally be married," I say as I press *Play* to the first movie that my mother picks out.

"I am so happy for you, Katie. I love Eli, and he has been definitely worth the wait."

Nodding in agreement, I am about to say something about him when the movie screen takes over. *Marrying a Murderer* flashes on the screen. "What in the world is this? I thought you rented a romantic comedy?" I stop the DVD and eject it from the player.

"Oh, I thought it was. Never mind, I'll return it. Put the next one in."

She shrugs, deep into brushing Dolly's adorable little poofy hair and inciting yawns from all of us. I scatter all the discs out that she rented, and there are many of them. She had gotten quite a few since she wants to watch them while we are away.

"Okay, how about *True Crime and Wedding Chimes*? Or better yet, *Honeymoon Hit: The True Story of a Wife Gone Dead*?

I sift through the rest and blindly pick up a random title. "Really? *Three Hots and a Marital Cot: The Story of the Wedding Bell Stranglers.* "I can't watch any of these, mother."

"You're so sensitive! Fine, put in one of yours," she laughs, knowing well that none of them are appropriate.

Thankfully, I had picked one of my own before she started her selections and popped one in the player. "Cheesy romcom, anyone?"

A couple appears on the screen, and the words splash above them: *'Barking Up the Wrong Tree,'* and a dog can be heard in the background. The couple are at a park, each with a small dog leashed up beside them.

"Boy, this feels. . . familiar somehow. Have we seen this, Katie?" She is taking slow bites of her cheese puffs, and I had stopped mine altogether.

"I don't think so. I mean, it's a new release. I think we would've remembered if we had."

The couple is now getting into some *hijinks* with their dogs as they finally meet, when each dog runs around them, forcing them to press together as they are now the mayflower pole to the leashes.

My phone buzzes; it's a text from Eli.

We are about to start our dinner fellowship here at the house. I just wanted to say that we'll see you at the chapel tomorrow. (groom emoji) (dog emoji)

"Who is that?" My mom looks at me over her readers and smiles, knowing it is something sweet from Eli.

"It's Eli, saying he will see me tomorrow at the wedding." I blush, relishing the words. *Only one more sleep until I'm his wife.*

"That reminds me, I better check in with your father and Edward. His suit needs to be pressed very specifically, and I don't want your father messing it up."

My mother and I decide she will stay with me tonight, and we will have a few people over to play board games and gush about tomorrow.

"Oh, and don't let me forget. He brought Grandma Pathy's earrings for you to wear."

"Dad is wearing a suit? I thought you said he is wearing the slacks with that dress shirt he bought for the clown comedy act in Vegas."

"No, Katie. *Edward's* suit. Its custom made, very delicate materials."

She makes a phone call, and I take a few minutes to look at my wedding dress one more time as it hangs from the rod of my closet and say a prayer.

"Dear Jesus,
Lord willing, I will marry Eli tomorrow.
I thank You so very much for all of this happening.

Your timing makes so much sense, and I wouldn't have wanted to be with anyone else.
Thank you, Jesus!
In your name,
Amen."

"Did you hear back from Dr. Brand yet, Katie?"

"Yes." I sigh, sharing with her the disappointing exam results and the side effects of the condition, including possible infertility.

"God is bigger than our illness, Katie. If you are meant to bring a child into this world, you will. There's nothing in life we need to worry about because it's all been planned out for us, in advance, by our all-knowing and loving God. Isn't that a relief?"

And it is. I love to hear the reassurance.

The doorbell rings, and I can hear the voices of Samantha, Judy, and Jenna floating throughout the apartment. I run out to the living room to see that they have brought bags of snacks, bridal magazines, and Jenna has a big train case she sets on the counter.

"I thought we could do pedicures! I have everything we need for a professional look."

I cheered at the idea. "I love that! Yes, please. My feet are crazy!"

She opens up the kit, and my mother sees something she likes.

"Jenna, what's this 'foot peel'? Do I need that?"

Jenna giggles and explains how it is a product that is *all the rage* online, but in reality, your foot sheds for two weeks.

"Katie will not be using that right before her wedding!" Everyone roars with the imagery of me hiding my feet from my new husband.

"I've just had my footsies done after my last visit to the podiatrist, but my hands need some color. Do you have any corals or oranges, Jenna?"

Judy had come with bare nails—something I wasn't sure that I'd ever seen on her, as they usually match her outfits.

"Oh yes, let's see what I have. Hmm. . . *Dragon's Breath'* reddish-orange, *Mermaid Mischief* 'coral, and then there's this pretty yellowish-orange, *Do I Look Fat in These Pants?'* Which one do you like?"

After a moment of silence, we all bust up laughing at how serious Jenna is about the nail polish names until she joins in, laughing the hardest.

"I think I'll go with *Mermaid Mischief,* dear. Can't go wrong with coral."

Jenna hands Judy the bottle, and she sits down at the kitchen table where my mother sets down a mat for her to use and turns up the dimmer on the chandelier so we can see better.

"Judy, may I do the honors? You have the perfect nail beds. I'd love to see what yours are like to paint."

Judy agrees to let my mother do her manicure as she takes the chair next to hers.

Jenna turns to me, motioning for me to choose my color.

"I have weird feet, but they look better with darker shades of polish." I keep my voice down, not wanting to make it a big deal as I ask for a dark red.

"You mean *blood red,* Katie."

My mother is now standing at my shoulder, holding a nail file as she exaggeratedly points to a red so dark, it's almost black.

"This is a lovely shade but maybe go a little lighter. Ah, like this. See? It's more of a *splatter.*"

We all settle on our colors, and Jenna helps oversee our techniques and thankfully steps in to help me when it is time to do the painting. Before she starts, she slips little toe separators onto my feet that make them look webbed. I look around the room, and everyone is wearing them. She does an amazing job, topping it off with a clear coat of sparkle.

"How did you do that so perfectly? I love it, thank you, Jenna!"

I try to get up, but she shakes her head. "You've got to stay put until they dry."

So, I sit there for the rest of the evening while enjoying the time watching movies, discussing my honeymoon plans, and chatting about the fact that tomorrow my world is changing.

That night, I dream of our wedding.

I am standing outside the doors of the church, which are about to dramatically open, revealing a small room and a door I have to enter before walking down the aisle. Doves are dramatically released, but since there is a room in the way, only I see them. I am not even sure who has the doves, but that is neither here nor there.

I look down at my dress, which is the same one I have bought, except in tie-dye.

"Eli is going to love this on me."

As I reach for the doorknob to walk down the aisle, my flip-flop comes off of my foot, but my dress skirt has now tripled in volume, so while I can feel the sandal, I can't find my feet to put it back on. I walk down the aisle with one flip-flop, except the pews are filled with the cats I've been grooming at the animal shelter, and at the end of the aisle is a giant frisbee, ready for me to marry while the guy from the slip-on veneer's commercial is ready to officiate.

He is smiling ear to ear; his lips once again stuck on his teeth.

"What do your real teeth look like?" I ask, and the music stops. It is an instrument that I don't recognize anyway; nowhere near a wedding march; more of a beat I'd hear at a Zumba class.

"They aren't too good, I'm afraid." He reaches up to remove the veneers, but I wave it off.

"Don't worry about it. Just marry us, will you?" I look back at the giant green frisbee I am now standing in front of and smile.

Opening my eyes, I feel my face immediately redden with shock. Today is the day. . . and what in the world was that dream? The biggest surprise was the footwear. I could never marry in *flip flops*; I could barely walk in them, let alone walk down an aisle filled with all the animals I've helped care for. It has to be the least reliable excuse for a *shoe* I've ever heard of, and I can't help but wonder if a kindergartener came up with that name. But it is superior to what my father refers to them as: *thongs.*

Though times have changed, my father has never reconsidered what he called them, to my horror. Imagine being a twelve-year-old girl in the heyday of a special "new" underwear craze. Before this garment went mainstream, we had the option of looking like we had four butts or were wearing our grandmother's girdle. But moms across America saw this new triangle shaped fabric as something reserved only for harlots and Europeans. None of that mattered, though, when I had one of my male school friends over for homework, and my father hollered out, "Where is my thong?"

It didn't matter that he was holding one foam *shoe* in his right hand, looking for the match to the pair, as my friend from school, whom I was hoping would fall madly in love with me and slip a promise ring on my chubby tween finger, now thought we were some sort of family made up of perverts.

None of that matters now. All of my years of looking, hoping, and praying for the right partner are finally coming to a close as, Lord willing, in just a few hours, I will be Mrs. Katie Skatey.

I reach over and tap the light on my alarm and turn it off. What used to be a very rude, inconsiderate beeping noise is now a fancy type of light. It slowly will start to shine on my face, like the sun will, if it ever comes out here. It turns on at seven in the morning, but this morning, I am already awake, thinking about the ceremony, the hotel reservation, the plane tickets, the traveling. . . But there is another thing on my mind, in addition to all of the above: *Dolly.*

We've become inseparable. She's my little sidekick everywhere I go, and since my boss Frank kept his word about converting our old conference room into a pet daycare, there hasn't been much time I've been away from her.

I've found her personality to be so much like my own. At work, it's an unspoken agreement that we all go check on our pets every hour on the hour. Or as Chaz says, "I'm going to make a drive by," meaning he walks to the water cooler the long way, to be sure he passes the glass daycare. Bringing her to work has also given me a chance to connect with my coworkers on a level I never have before.

Overall, Dolly has improved my work life beyond imagination; she gives me an edge. But by far, the biggest difference at work has been in Chaz. I've really enjoyed watching the changes in him since he adopted his Persian cat, Reginald.

He seems more relaxed, and it may have been the rumors of my having a guy now, but he immediately began to act more respectful towards myself and the other ladies in the office. He is also, it seems, happier. I always thought deep down he must be lonely to put up such a front. The day I returned to the office after my road trip to visit my parents, Chaz was drinking out of a coffee mug that read, *Cat Dad,* and he would bring Reginald to work wearing miniature matching neckties.

Chaz's once-mysterious home life is also slowly unfolding through pictures he shares every Monday morning of his cat. Our meetings now hold a few minutes at the end where we share something personal if we want. It is completely elective, and people just share something about their pets or plants, if they still don't have the former (ahem, *Jonathan).*

One Monday, Chaz shared a picture of his mother holding Reginald. "We discovered Reggie likes celery. We were cutting some up for a veggie tray when he took off with a piece!"

The group snickered and commented on what "people" food their pets liked.

While I had never pictured Chaz as the type that would hang out with his parents, let alone have a sweet relationship with his mother, that was when I started to see the softer side of him. If Samantha wasn't already in a relationship with Mitchell, I'd have given her a glowing half-thumbs up on this guy. I wondered if Chaz lived with his parents, or they lived with him which also made sense as he was a moderately successful attorney with older parents. Either way, it was sweet.

It reminded me of the time when I had just turned 18 and was chatting with a good-looking guy online. He only had one profile picture; half of his face was covered by something "cool;" the other half with dark *emo* hair.

He lived several states away, but we had some sort of *online* "felationship" going, more so in my head than in reality. He was a few years older than me, but since it was still an innocent friendship, I didn't think it was important. But when we finally made it to the phone call territory, our phone calls kept dropping right as an elderly woman's voice would call out his name.

"Sorry, I have a bad connection."

"In that big city you live in, I assumed connectivity would be rather good. Especially on a landline."

Cell phones had just started taking off. I'd only been texting a few days at this point, and my flip phone had zero internet capabilities.

"You'd be surprised. There's a really bad—".

"Jeffrey?" the woman's older, strained voice called again. *Click.*

He would call me back a few minutes later.

"Sorry again. Anyway, what were we talking about?"

"You were telling me about your large apartment you rent. How it's so nice to live alone and definitely not with your mother."

"Oh, was I? Right. Yes, I certainly don't live with my mother at twenty-three-years old, haha! Can you imagine? What would you think of that if a guy my age did?"

"I wouldn't think anything of it. I still live with my parents too. I'd be more concerned about any dishonesty."

"Right, right. Yeah, okay. Well, the thing is—,".

"Jeffrey? The macaroni is ready."

This time he didn't hang up.

"Okay, thanks... *Mom.*" *Silence.*

"Katie?" he asked, sheepishly.

"Yeah, Jeffrey?"

"Uhm... never mind."

Click.

That was the end of that "relationship."

Chapter 14
Something Borrowed, Something Chewed
Katie

I prop myself up on my pillows and look over to Dolly. She is just wrestling out of her blanket as we both keep to a similar schedule.

"Good morning, sweetie." I cheer at her, quietly, but then I hear my mother come into the apartment, like we agreed she would. At first, she shuts the door softly, trying not to wake me. My ears perk up at the sound of a slow trickle of water coming out of the sink. *Good,* I think, *she's making coffee.*

Just then, I hear a crash, followed by a scream. I jump out of bed, rip my bedroom door open, and run to the kitchen to find my mother on the floor.

"Oh my! Are you OKAY?" I nearly scream out to her as she nods.

"I spilled a little water, that's all. I just landed a little hard on my rear end." She sits up as I help her and starts to laugh. "This reminds me of your first job, Katie."

Dolly peeks around the corner, seeing if the coast is clear for her to come out.

"Come here, Dolly. She's fine; let's take you outside." I pick Dolly up and place her on her grass pad on the patio.

"How does it remind you of the ice cream parlor?" I shake my head.

"That one night I picked you up from work, why, you looked like you'd seen a ghost!" She starts laughing hysterically and now has tears falling from her eyes.

I am starting to remember, but for nostalgia's sake, I prompt her to tell it as she recalls. "Go on," I smile and bring Dolly back in after she has used her grass pad, holding her.

"I asked you what was wrong, and you said you forgot to put the wet floor sign up after mopping the manager's office." She is now in a coughing fit. "Papers-scattered-everywhere," choking out the words, "but your boss is too cool to tell anyone he fell."

Ah, yes. Darren. One minute he was carrying a stack of important readings to his desk, the next moment the papers were flying through the air. For the next month, whenever he thought no one was looking, he had a limp but never confessed to his falling. I felt terrible and was very diligent after that about the sign placement, mostly because I like to see the *'dance of the wet floors'* people perform when they think their necks depend on it. It's more than a tiptoeing; it's a kind of a mashup between playing *Hot Potato* and the *Floor is Lava.*

Once she is up, her legs aren't quite moving right, and I am worried she will need to go to the doctor.

"No, Katie. I just need to walk this off is all. The dogs will keep me plenty active this week; for now, I just need my girdle. Yes, that will straighten me out. It's time we start getting ready for the wedding" She grins ear to ear, and my heart leaps.

*****

The morning goes by in a flash. I am so nervous, I can barely finish a cup of coffee, but I don't need any help in the energy department. I think I woke up with jitters.

Julie had set up a room for us to use at the church to get dressed in, so I put on a button-up shirt, leggings, and slip-on shoes and then sit down and let my mother help me with my hair and makeup.

After I am done up, I can't remember a time when I've ever felt more beautiful. My mother does her hair and makeup while I put

Dolly's hair up in two pigtails with purple bows. It is time to leave now!

My mother reminds me at the last minute to grab my suitcase from Audrey out of the hallway closet, and I can't help but feel a little emotional.

Once we got to the church, I am elated to see that Judy, Pastor Bill, and Julie are already there. They have transformed the large reception room into the wedding venue of my dreams. All our regular brown tables have been covered in white linens, each topped with a lace runner and a vase full of hyacinth flowers which let out a beautiful, light fragrance.

"I hope you like it my dear," Judy says as she hugs me.

"I absolutely love it. Thank you. I'm so touched."

"You better go get ready now. We will finish up here. I brought my infamous ambrosia, and I better go check on it."

"I can't wait." I beam ear to ear, hugging her once more before running off into the dressing room.

While we had planned to only serve dessert, my loved one's have other plans. They put together a simple but delicious brunch consisting of quiche and fresh fruit, along with a few sides including Judy's most loved ambrosia. I feel beyond blessed to have my church family.

When we go into the dressing room, my mother covers my hair once again in a coating of hairspray, "for good measure," and once it is practically immobilized, we feel confident it will last the ceremony. It is a chilly, wet day, and we all feel the cool air, so I have a blanket over me until it is time to get dressed.

As I step into my gown, now on the day I will marry, I feel the tears coming, and it is everything I can do to get a grip and not ruin my makeup.

"Dear Jesus,
Thank You."

"Ready for me to button you up?" My mother steps over, also appearing to be choking up.

"Yes, please." I take a deep breath, closing my eyes, and thinking of the handsome hunk I am about to kiss on the altar. Though we have each kissed others before, we decided to save our first kiss for today. I haven't told anyone that, as it is personal, but the thought of kissing him is making me feel faint and also making me feel like brushing my teeth again, for the *third* time this morning.

Once I am buttoned up, I go to the small sink in the corner, squeezing out some toothpaste onto my brush.

"Again, Katie? Don't you have any *Binaca?*" She pulls out a miniature aerosol can from her pocket and shakes it up like spray paint. "Here, you can have this."

I already have my mouth full of blue minty paste but take it anyway.

"Just don't get it mixed up with your can of mace."

"I'll try not to. Thanks." I smile. I am so nervous now. I need baby powder on my hands, underarms, feet, behind the knees, eyelids, forehead, and upper lip.

"I think it's about time. Let me go get the ladies for our prayer and then we will be ready."

The women in my life all scatter into the room and gather around, each giving me a warm embrace and words of love before we all take hands in a group prayer, led by Julie. My heart skips knowing Eli is doing the same shortly with Pastor Bill and his father, friends, and family.

"Dear Heavenly Father,
We thank You for the beautiful love between Katie and Eli.
I pray that You bless their union. May they always forgive one another,
show patience, kindness, and respect to each other,
but above all, always seek You first.
In Your name,
Amen."

"Amen. Thank you all so much," I speak, my words being followed by a beautiful piano song.

"It's time, Katie."

I am led down a hallway that wraps around the front of the church and has beautiful windows letting a gentle amount of daylight in. My shoes tap on the tile floors and with every step, I feel a little more like I am floating. My dress sways, and instead of a bouquet, I am holding Dolly. *Wait, Dolly?*

"Where is my bouquet?" I suddenly panic.

My mother shows me it is in her hand. "Right here, Katie."

Dolly is wearing a little purple dress, and I exchange her with my mother for the handpicked purple flowers, as I step into the aisle to walk towards my groom, just as the music picks up.

Eli's face reveals a plethora of emotions. He has small tears forming in his eyes, and he mouths a *"Wow"* as he looks at me in my gown. He looks gorgeous in his dark gray suit and when I reach him, I can feel Jenna reach for my bouquet and Eli's hands taking mine, giving the back of my hand a kiss, and I thank the Lord for this day.

Pastor Bill gives the guests permission to take a seat as he starts the vows.

"Do you, Eli, take Katie to be your lawfully wedded wife, to have and to hold, from this day forward, for better or for worse, for richer or for poorer, in sickness and in health, to love and to cherish, as long as you both shall live, even when the fur flies and the leash gets tangled?"

We all giggle at the last bit, and Eli looks me in the eyes and answers.

"Yes, I do."

Pastor Bill turns to me and repeats the same vows.

"I do." My face hurts from smiling.

"I now pronounce you husband and wife. Eli, you may kiss your bride."

When the vows are spoken, and we both excitedly agree to them, Eli embraces me for our first kiss, and now we are married. His pillowy lips meet mine with relief, as I've dreamt of this day for months, and it feels like the most natural thing in the world. I am blessed.

After the ceremony, our friends and family gather around us, giving good wishes, and we move into the banquet hall. Somewhere in between the day, Pastor Bill and Julie have hung up beautiful twinkling lights from the ceiling and dimmed the overhead bulbs. It is magical. Eli and I steal one more kiss before he leads me into the room.

"After you, Mrs. Skatey." Eli holds my hand as we walk inside the reception, after everyone else has sat down. They cheer for us again, and Jenna encourages me to toss the bouquet. I laugh as Eli nods in agreement.

"We had a few ideas for this tradition." Eli is laughing as he speaks. "Instead of tossing a bouquet, we thought my bride should toss this."

He pulls out the miniature, neon green frisbee that he hit me in the head with at our first meeting. It is utterly painless, weighing hardly anything; besides, the point is for a bridesmaid to catch it, not get hit. Our guests laugh as all the non-married women in the room gather in the center of the room.

"Alright, ladies. In avoiding a lawsuit, my eyes will be closed, so everyone should do what they can to shield the innocent."

Judy cheers as she moves to the front of the women waiting for the frisbee. I cover my eyes with my left hand and give it a gentle toss, hearing cheers from the group. When I uncover my eyes, Samantha is holding the frisbee.

"I didn't get hit in the head; does it still count?"

Everyone laughs as we go around the room taking pictures with our guests while they enjoy the beautiful brunch spread, fizzy sparkling drinks, and finally, cake. When we eventually sit down at the table reserved just for us, speeches begin. Butterflies start playing the drums in my stomach as I know that my mother will be among them.

Eli's father, Pete, starts it off. He taps the microphone three times and makes sure it is on, as we all duck and cover, realizing it is on full blast. Pastor Bill runs to the audio station and sets it to a much better level.

"Hello all, I'm Eli's father, Pete, for those who don't know me. Marsha and I couldn't be happier at this wonderful union, and we're overjoyed to gain a daughter. And a racquetball partner." He nods to my father, who salutes back.

"I hereby declare our game yesterday a tie, by the way. I do not accept that you beat me with my own sneaky move. Anyhow," he clears his throat, "thank you Eli for choosing such a wonderful woman to join our family. And thank you Katie, for having parents that we like so very much."

Everyone laughs.

Audrey and her darling son, Connor, say a few words about the first time they all met me.

"My uncle threw the frisbee, and I didn't know where it went."   Giggles erupt.

"I ran around looking and there it was, next to a woman. I hoped it didn't hit her, but I think it did."

Connor holds the frisbee and re-enacts the infamous event that introduced us.

Once he is done speaking, and we all cheer and clap, my mother stands up and makes her way to the microphone. My stomach clenches.

"On behalf of my daughter, I'd like to thank you all for not just showing up today, but for showing up in life. This room is proof of the love you all have for my daughter and my new son, and this mother thanks you."

I let out the breath I am holding. So far, so good. She goes on.

"Indeed, this is a special day, one I know many of us didn't think we'd ever see: Katie wearing *white* after Labor Day. A cardinal sin it may not be, but in some cultures, it is a capital offense."

Giggles come from the crowd, and I nervously laugh at her innocent joke.

"Today, my daughter Katie is marrying the love of her life, Eli, after she went out on a limb and adopted a precious dog. Isn't it incredible how the Lord weaves our stories together? He waited for her to take a leap of faith, and in that leap, her head met a green plastic frisbee."

She pulls the frisbee out of her pocket and holds it up like it is *EXHIBIT A.* "So, here's to the Skatey's! May your lives be joyful. May the hardships bring you closer together, and the troubles strengthen your faith in God. May the good moments, the number of rescue dogs, and the trips to visit your in-laws be plentiful, always. Congratulations to the happy couple!"

"That was lovely, actually," I whisper to Eli who nods in agreement. I mouth to my mother, 'thank you,' but she purses together her lips and looks away. I have a feeling more is coming.

Someone wheels into the room with a projector on a table, causing my heart to rapidly sink. My mother reaches for a rope handle that is behind the balloon arch, pulling it down. I stand, contemplating if I were to heroically stop this madness from happening, but then the lights go out, and Eli grabs my hand in his.

"It's going to be okay. You can't get rid of me now; it's a legally binding marriage." He winks.

I only wish I had the same confidence he has at this very moment.

"I took the liberty to put together a little slideshow of Katie's life, and a brief history of Eli, thanks to his wonderful mom and dad." She gives them a short round of applause and begins.

"Maybe this won't be so bad after all?" I whisper to Eli, who has his arm around me now for moral support.

I am wrong. So, so wrong.

"Aww." The attendees collectively giggle at the first round of baby pictures. I'd forgotten to mention to Eli just what I looked like back then.

"Katie was a very round baby, as you can all tell. In fact, the hospital said they'd never seen a fatter infant!"

Murmurs grow to loud laughter.

"No, you're thinking of Jabba the Hutt."

Who said that? I feel mortified to the point I was ready for the teenage awkward years. As if in cue, my mother announced it.

"Then she grew up into this silly girl."

No, no, no!

"Is that. . . face paint, Katie?"

I nod, looking into the now genuinely concerned eyes of my handsome *husband.* My mother continues.

"She went through a phase where she only wanted to go out in public after she'd 'put her face on,' just like mom, but you can see in this picture especially—oh, where is it?" The pictures keep getting worse and worse, and more zoomed in. "Here it is!"

My face, in all my dark maroon blush and orange foundation glory, is covering the entire screen.

"She's always been a beauty."

Everyone laughs, thinking it is a joke, but the look on my mother's face reveals it isn't meant to be. And now she is flipping through that segment faster, completely skipping over my "blonde" attempts.

"This is the phase I call, 'baby fat to *baby goth*.'"

A picture of me in all black clothing with my hair yanked behind me in a slicked back ponytail comes on. The laughter hasn't stopped.

"Then, she very innocently dived into the dating world."

My head goes into my hands, and I feel tears forming behind my eyes.

"Of course, nobody was good enough for mother bear here."

A few claps come from the crowd as she documents every date I've ever been on. I wasn't aware that any of these photos existed, and more than one of them looked like they were taken from behind shrubbery. The preteen crushes, the middle school dance photos, and worst of all, the teenager who lived down the street: a picture of him and me on our front porch.

"I asked the neighbor kid to come say hello to Katie one time to give her a thrill. Of course, he wanted to take her to the movies, but I said no."

What? The neighborhood heartthrob wanted to take me on a date, and my mother had said no?

"But Katie never settled for anything less than prince charming. Her trust in the Lord and His timing was unwavering. She knew that she would meet her perfect partner right when she was supposed to and that's exactly what happened."

Our guests clap, as the pictures change from my cringy high school snaps to an adorable, normal-sized baby boy.

"His mother told me his favorite baby food was mashed bananas. Katie, take notes."

Eli and I laugh as the pictures change. A peewee football team covers the screen, followed by t-ball, basketball, track, and soccer.

"Eli had quite the athletic childhood."

A stark contrast to mine.

"Here, he is standing next to his trophy wall. Exceptionally good genetics to pass down. . . Don't you all agree?"

Eli nervously laughs and squeezes my shoulder.

The next few minutes go by fast since I am no longer the subject up for sharing, but the room sounds like someone has a sitcom laugh track. Every time my mother speaks, the crowd cackles.

"Here's Eli after a miscommunication at the mall hair salon. May we all learn the lesson young, that you *never* describe your desired look as a little long but a little short."

A photo of Eli with red, teary eyes and a botched *mullet-like* haircut comes up. Eli is a good sport about it, and I laugh a little *too* hard.

"Now, I've saved something *really* special for the end."

Here we go.

"My friends down at the crime lab, well, they created a few images of what Katie and Eli's children might look like."

I hold my breath and give a wide-eyed look to Eli, and he shrugs his shoulders as we wait for the image to pop up. Admittedly, I am curious what the results will be.

"Aren't those just the sweetest faces you've ever seen?"

I let out a roar of laughter with the rest of our guests as a basket full of miniature brown poodles, which are identical to Dolly and Carter, take over the screen.

"I hope you join me in wishing the couple a lifetime of happiness and *oodles of poodles!*"

The lights come back on as she wheels away the projector and then some soft music starts playing. Eli stands, taking my hand and leads me onto the dance floor. He can feel my nerves as everyone is watching.

"May I have this dance, Mrs. Skatey?"

I nod, smiling back and feel a similar feeling to when I adopted Dolly months ago. I am going to stop overthinking and instead, lean into the unknown. Dancing in front of our guests is only scary if I let it be. Thankfully, it is a slow, smooth dance that only requires our swaying side to side. And towards the end of the song, a rhythmic beat starts, and everyone joins us on the dance floor, to my delight.

A few songs in, I am breathless and thirsty. I look over to my mother who is standing next to the stroller with Dolly and Carter inside, clapping along and singing to them. My father is in a full-arm cast with Edward on his lap. My mother was spot on with Edward's custom suit. He looks impeccable, including his coordinating muzzle. I feel so much joy wash over me.

More dancing, decadent buttercream frosted cake, and too many sparkling ciders later, everyone starts winding down as the festivities come to their natural close. We say goodbye to our families and friends, and help my parents load the dogs into the car. When I ask my father about his cast, he mumbles something about it being used as a preventative measure, as Edward seems to just go after his left arm—that it is just a dummy cast that can be removed. Edward and my father will be staying with my mother for a few days at my apartment before going back home, as he needs to return to work, and she assures me their elaborate plan of keeping Edward in the kitchen with a baby gate will be flawless. I hug them both goodbye and thank my mother again for all she did for the wedding and now babysitting.

"Don't worry about a thing, Katie. Dolly and Carter will be so spoiled, they won't even have time to wonder about mom and dad. This is what grandma's dream of."

I hug her again and give each dog a kiss and hug, and Eli does the same.

"Check in with me if you want, but not too often. This is about you two." She slides my suitcase out of the back seat and rolls it over to Eli. "I almost forgot," she smiles, and I know I am about to brace for a rough landing. "I'll be tracking both of your locations." She holds up her phone and shows a new icon with Eli's face on it.

"How reassuring," Eli laughs, putting his arm around me.

We say our goodbyes, and Eli leads me to his car where he puts my suitcase into, and he drives us to a beautiful hotel that overlooks the city. At check in, we receive many congratulations based on our attire. They ask us about checkout, but Eli lets them know we'll be up at dawn to depart for our honeymoon.

The bellhop leads us to our room, opens the door, and slides our luggage inside before spinning on his heels and disappearing down the hallway. Eli looks at me, smiles, and in one fluid movement, scoops me up and carries me over the threshold. "It's tradition," he laughs as he sits me back down, but not before kissing me. He shuts the door behind us, and I am overwhelmed with the excitement of starting our lives together.

Chapter 15
Furever Starts Now
Carolyn

The sign hasn't even been hammered in yet when we get our first official offer.

The real estate agent has had a mallet in her hand for about thirty seconds when a neighbor next door walks over, asking for details about our house.

"Nearly entirely gutted and remodeled. Gorgeous original hardwood floors that have been refinished. Crown molding installed to the era of the home, new fixtures, and appliances. Two bedrooms, one bath; it's the perfect starter home or investment opportunity."

I watch as she hands him a neatly folded brochure with bright colored photos and the details listed that she just recited from memory. She is *good*. We know her from the gym, and I can see that we made the right call already.

"I'd like to make an offer. I have a mother who needs somewhere to live that isn't my second bedroom. I love her, but she acts like I'm living under her rule. I invited her to live with me, and I'm in my fifties, for crying out loud! Don't tell my husband, or heck, he'll probably agree, but I'll mortgage my house just to put her in this."

The sale moves at a rapid pace when our neighbor does in fact take out a second mortgage and secures a hefty down payment. We have a thirty-day close, which is plenty of time to paint the porch. To Micah's delight, the home inspection comes back swimmingly, as I knew it would. Now, with the profits of his hard labor, we can ride off into the sunset of Wyoming with peace of mind knowing we have a little nest egg.

Katie and Eli's wedding was darling. They looked so happy, and we are both so elated for them, especially having since found each other. As they prepared to leave for an Alaskan honeymoon, Micah asked me where I wanted to honeymoon.

"To be honest, I didn't even think about a honeymoon. Plus, now we have the extra dogs. I mean, it's not like we can get Katie's mom to babysit them, too, right? Wyoming is my honeymoon." I kiss him, thanking him for not forgetting about it, even though I had.

"Wow." Micah leans back and puts his hands over his head. "Where did you come from, dream girl?"

I put my head on his shoulder.

"Why don't we get settled in Wyoming, and then take one from there? My mom would love to watch the dogs. Besides, that little airport goes to a lot of bigger airports. We can go anywhere in the world."

"Anywhere?"

"Anywhere my bride wants. I promise."

Chapter 16
Honeymoon Unleashed
Katie

The phone rings, illuminating the dark room with a red flashing light, as if we can't hear its blaring noise. Eli, reaching for it, answers with a raspy, morning voice.

"Hello?"

I can hear the perky voice on the other end of the line.

"This is your wakeup call, Mr. Skatey."

Eli sits up. "Thank you very much."

Hanging up the phone, he leans over to me and says it is time for our future to begin, and for a moment, I just lay there, relishing the last few seconds of the first time waking up to my new husband.

We save ourselves about twenty minutes to get ready in the room before heading to the car. I pull my suitcase up on the bed and unzip it, and thankfully, the outfit I had planned to wear on the plane is right on top. *Audrey thought of everything.* Around noon today, she will be receiving a delivery from a florist from me, and I cannot wait until she gets it and knows how much I appreciate her.

The hotel front desk will hold onto my wedding dress, and my mother will pick it up later. All the details are arranged, and there is nothing left to worry about.

Once I don my darling airport outfit, Eli lets out a low whistle and can't stop complimenting my look. "You look so *high fashion,* Mrs. Skatey."

I blush and thank him, noticing my outfit of distressed denim, a long henley with layered plaid flannel, and wedge boots are identical to his henley, plaid, and jeans.

"We kind of match."

I'm not sure how I feel about that. Sure, when it happens with Dolly, we get nothing but compliments. But a man and woman matching? Thankfully, we don't look like we could be related, or people might think we are twins.

"You mean, *we go together,"* He winks and picks up our suitcases, as we start our journey to Alaska.

After an exceedingly lengthy line through TSA, and sign after sign discouraging the petting of the police dogs, we get a few coffees and a light breakfast while we meander to our gate. At takeoff, Eli puts his hand on mine. I may have had my eyes closed and had just been loudly reciting Psalm 23, but while my adventurous husband realizes I am a little fearful of flying, I find his presence comforting. It is either that or the chamomile tea the flight attendant gave me, but after a few minutes I doze off, only waking when the plane is on its final descent.

"Good morning," Eli kisses my forehead when he sees I've awakened.

"Oh my. . . I'm sorry. The last few weeks just caught up to me all at once." I yawn but admittedly feel so refreshed and *relieved* the plane ride will soon be over. I lean on his shoulder and look out of his window. I have never seen anything so beautiful—snowy mountain caps scattered across the landscape, dotted with frozen lakes, and the biggest pine trees I've ever seen. It also looks very, very cold as the window has a little bit of frost accumulated on it. I worry I've not brought enough layers for my winter honeymoon but remember the brochure for our bed and breakfast resort offers dog mushing outfits to borrow as well.

"It's absolutely breathtaking," I smile at Eli who nods to me in agreement. "Can we see the resort from here?"

Eli pulls out a map in his pocket, scanning it and looking back at the mountains. "I can't be sure, but it might be that right there. We are close enough to the airport that location makes sense. Plus, it has that giant archway."

I look at what he is pointing at and gasp. The plane is getting lower, so we seem to be going faster as it whizzes by, but before it leaves from my view, I see a beautiful, red roofed lodge nestled in the oversized trees with smokestacks billowing out from the stone chimneys. A sense of coziness takes over as I picture us soon to be sipping hot chocolate in front of our fireplace in the honeymoon suite.

After landing, we wait at the carousel for our luggage, but thankfully, it is the first to unload.

"That almost never happens," Eli laughs, recounting a story from when he lost his luggage for seven days, only to be located once he returned home. "I got a lot of wear out of the airport gift shop clothing."

"That explains that outfit you have that says *Key West* head-to-toe," I tease.

"No, you know I just really like tie dye," he smiles and tightens his grip around my shoulder, kissing my hair. "My luggage was lost when I went to San Antonio for work training."

He releases his arm around me as we slide our luggage through the exit doors and look for transportation. If I ever felt like I was a foreigner, it was now as I look around in awe of the mountains that are all around us in the distance. The cold temperature is refreshing and jolts my senses. There is fresh snow on the ground and people are out sweeping and salting the walks.

The resort had said there would be someone there waiting to pick us up.

A plain colored van, void of logos pulls up. "This must be us." Eli confidently strides to the vehicle.

"Why would the hotels use that sort of vehicle to pick up passengers from the airport?" I ask aloud. It is one of those angular, bulbous vans that inhibit thoughts of murderers and abductors.

Eli disagrees. "These are pretty high end, and standard, Katie. I'm sure this is our van. . ."

Eli laughs at my questioning the driver to show me his itinerary, and when he hands the paper to me, it does indeed have our names on it.

"Great. You just can never be too careful, is all."

"Why does this feel like a sneak peek of what traveling with your mother will be like?" He is grinning ear to ear.

"Okay, you're right. Her paranoia has just really rubbed off on me over the years."

We giggle to ourselves as the hotel shuttle takes a few quick turns and before we know it, we've made it to the hotel.

"Hello, sir. We are the Skatey's. And you are?"

The man nods and pulls up the lanyard he is wearing that hide inside his long beard that reads off the name of the hotel, his photo, and his name, *Bob Foot.*

"The name is Bob. Most folks call me Footy." He grins a surprisingly nice, white smile, and I quickly ask forgiveness under my breath for being so quick to assume he would be toothless.

"Nice to meet you, Footy. I'm Eli and this is my wife, Katie."

A shockwave goes down my entire body as I hear Eli call me his wife out in the wild. It settles in, all at once, that I am officially married, and it is real. I take his hand as Footy loads up our luggage in the back, and he opens the doors for us to slide into the bucket seats.

Footy uses his turning signal, and we turn into a beautiful, snowy village that has a large wooden archway reading *Everwood.*

Eli whispers to me, "Isn't this fun?" as he smiles ear to ear. looking around as it starts to gently snow. The sun is still out, and it sparkles all around us. It truly is magical, and I decide for this very moment, I want to take this in and see its beauty rather than the dangers that may or may not be there.

The ride takes less than ten minutes as Footy gently slows the vehicle into a small road that unveils our beautiful ski resort. It is the one we saw from the plane, and up close we can see that inside the floor to ceiling windows, they have a huge fireplace with big timbers roaring to life inside.

Footy parks under the awning marked, *Unloading Zone* and swiftly gets out, retrieves our luggage, and opens the doors. The air feels even colder now, and I hope Audrey has packed me extra pairs of the thermals I can wear under my clothes. Footy opens the large, front door of the lodge, and we walk inside, greeted by the warmth of the fire. There is a woman at the desk who has two piping hot ciders for us. It is very welcoming, and we both go for them immediately.

"Thank you, Footy." Eli looks back at our driver and gives him a cash tip.

"It was my pleasure. I will see you folks again when you depart." Footy bows and goes back outside to his vehicle and drives off.

The elevator dings that we have made it to our floor, and the doors open. Eli is able to secure the honeymoon suite. When Eli opens the double doors to our room, we both gasp in amazement as the view is overlooking the stunning snowy mountain range, and we both run to the window. The light is hitting it right, and we feel like we are in a sparkling snow globe.

"Oh my! Do you see that?" I see a creature walking in the distance with large antlers.

"This all backs up to an elk refuge. I am hoping we can wake up to them bugling." The wonder in his eyes is charming, and his excitement is contagious.

"That sounds... lovely." I have never experienced anything like that, and it excites me.

"You're lovely," He gushes and kisses me.

At night we enjoy a beautiful candlelit dinner in the resort's gorgeous dining room. There are groups scattered around us, half in ski gear, the other half in casual wear. Layla, who explains she also moonlights as room service in the winter months, comes with a menu to make our selections. She makes suggestions, and she takes our order.

"Okay, so Eli will be getting the King Salmon, pan seared, and Katie?"

"I will take your suggestion and try the pan-fried Halibut, with panko coating."

She grins ear to ear. "It's my favorite way to have it prepared! I mean, I have had to get creative with what we have here in abundance in Alaska, and I know you'll love it. My whole family is in the fishing business, so there's not a day that goes by where something from the sea is not on our table. My other favorite is fried fish fingers. I'll have to get those for you next."

"Sounds very... appetizing!"

We all laugh as Layla explains they are like a fish stick. She takes our dinner menus and says Peter will be returning with the food shortly as she leaves.

There is a beautiful spread for dinner, and not just what we have ordered. They include freshly baked pumpernickel bread with honey butter, a savory salmon dip with salt crackers, and caviar. The last thing he places on our dining table is a flight of desserts. Our entrees are huge and piled high with multiple sides that include vegetables, couscous, and potatoes.

"I have to break it to you, husband."

Eli looks up, concerned at my tone.

"Keep this up, and I'm not fitting in that bathing suit you're so eager to see me in."

"Well, we better make the trip sooner than later, in that case." He smiles and winks at me.

I'm so glad he has a good sense of humor, I think to myself, as I take another bite of my scalloped potatoes.

Afterwards, they clear out our dishes and upon going back to our room, we are considering going to the outdoor hot tub. But when we reach our room, the phone is ringing. *Oh no,* I think. I have been so consumed with traveling and the hotel that I've forgotten to check in with my mother, and now she's calling. As Eli goes to answer the phone, I cringe. But it's not her.

"That was the front desk giving us an Aurora Borealis alert." He smiles, turns off the room lights, and we both run to the window again, faces pressed up against the glass. He puts his arm around me as we watch the colorful ribbons dance across the sky. I feel tears forming as I looked at God's perfect creation.

We watch the Northern Lights for what feels like hours, and though the sky has darkened shortly after our dinner is served, I feel energized. Only when Eli started yawning did the idea of getting some sleep return to me.

"It's nine," Eli laughs. "Feels like the middle of the night. I'm wiped."

I nod, now, too, yawning. "Hot tubbing will have to wait until tomorrow."

"Very true. I better check in and let my mother know we made it safe, then I'm going to change into my pajamas."

"To be honest, I want to hear what Dolly and Carter are up to also. I miss them a little. Tomorrow we will explore!"

Eli nods, "Oh, good. I know—it's so hard to be away from our little cuties. I might fall asleep the moment my head hits the pillow. Wake me if I do."

I laugh at my cute husband and go into the sitting area of our suite to make a phone call. My mother answers on the first ring.

"Hi, Katie. How is it there?"

"Hi! It's beautiful. We've been watching the northern lights all evening. We just ate a feast of seafood. It's just lovely here." I go on to tell her about the flight, the drive up to the hotel, and how beautiful the scenery is.

"Aww. I think that sounds amazing! Enjoy yourselves. We are doing wonderfully here. Carter and Dolly are going to be special guests on Mystery Maven tomorrow. But don't worry, I'll blur their faces to respect their privacy."

I let out a low laugh, my heart feeling full that my mother is having such a fun time with the dogs. But the mention of her show makes me remember something else. "Are you going to call Frank tomorrow? They have a Monday morning meeting, but he should be able to take your call any time after nine. . ." I trail off, not wanting to overly stress anything.

"Yes, I've already reached out, actually. Sent him a few wedding stills I snapped while rewatching the camcorder footage. He's taking me to coffee tomorrow to discuss."

"Oh, wow, that is—".

She cuts me off. "Okay, Katie, go enjoy your honeymoon. I'll text you after I meet with Frank. But don't worry about getting back to me right away. This is about you and Eli."

I smile. "Who is this and what have you done with my mother?" I can't believe she doesn't want me to check in with her every few hours like normal.

"I know you're safe with Eli. Besides, you'll be back here before we know it. Then, you two will be moving, looking for a job, and one day, a house. It's best to immerse yourself in these infrequent trips whenever you can. We are all fine here, and I know you are too. You've got a great head on your shoulders, Katie. I know you're not out traipsing through alleyways and knocking on strange doors with yards full of plastic flamingos with their heads cut off."

"How oddly specific. . . But, thank you. Okay, I better get going then. Text me after your meeting with Frank and talk to you soon."

We hang up the phone, and I sit there for a moment in complete amazement. My mother has never let up the reins until just now. It feels good, but I 'm also not sure if something else is going on. I hate to think about it, but I also hate to feel it. I am worried that my mother is feeling more troubled by that whole Kyle case. She just isn't acting like herself.

Katie's Words of Law
Duress
Doo-rĕs
Noun
When you hand a screaming toddler an iPad to silence them.

I go to my suitcase and find the silk pajamas that Audrey picked out and some thick wool socks because my feet are freezing. By the sound of Eli's snores, I am certain he won't see any fashion faux pas. I tiptoe to the bed and decide I will just let him sleep as it has been a long day. And shortly after my head hits the pillow, I, too, fall into a deep slumber.

The next morning, I awake to the sounds of the shower being turned on full blast. It is still dark in the room, but the sun doesn't rise this time of year until around eight in the morning, so it could still be a reasonable time. I roll over to look at the clock on Eli's nightstand, and it is flashing *12:00. Hmm. How weird—the clock must've become unplugged at some point, because I swear it was showing the correct time last night.*

Unless. . .

Maybe there had been a power outage. Or a surge, and it flicked off for just a moment, resetting the clocks. Seems like a reasonable thing, especially in this part of the world, during deep winter. *Unless it was intentional. What if the killer turned off all the lights, scoured the hotel looking for us, and is right outside our door as I lay here, about to meet him face to face.*

"Stop!" I nearly holler at my mind as it starts creeping towards some crazy, crime related reason. The water instantly shuts off.

"Katie?" Eli calls.

Dang it—he heard me acting crazy.

"Are you okay?"

"Yes, sorry. I was just. . . talking to myself."

Oops. The words slip out of my mouth faster than I have a chance to consider admitting that.

He snickers, and mumbles something like, "Okay, then."

I don't hear the water turn back on, so I decide to ask, "What time is it?"

"Sorry if I woke you. It's nearly seven in the morning. I accidentally unplugged the clock this morning trying to plug in my phone charger."

He walks out of the bathroom wearing the hotel robe and sheepishly smiles, motioning to the blinking light, and I act like I hadn't noticed.

"I'm famished. It must be the wintry weather and higher altitude. Shall I order room service for breakfast, Mrs. Skatey?"

"Yes, that would be wonderful, Mr. Skatey."

I have just enough time to shower and dress before they arrive with our food, and we watch the sunrise as we finish off the lovely breakfast spread in our room.

"Good choice for breakfast this morning, husband. Eggs Benedict is my favorite."

"Thank you, wife. I thought it sounded amazing with the smoked salmon. I don't know about you, but I'm ready to ski," Eli says as he drinks the last of his coffee.

Chapter 17
Love Can Be Ruff
Samantha

"Hey, Sam. Can we talk tonight? After you get off work." Mitchell's voice seems determined, as he rapidly fires off his question the moment I answer his call.

"Sure, where are you? Do you just want to come in here? It's a bit slow here and—".

He cuts me off. "No, no. It can wait. Shall we meet at, say, the little park near Pine Bluff House? That home turned into an art gallery."

"Oh, we've never been there before. Sure, you don't want to go to the Bark Park?"

I'm not sure why he is suggesting somewhere new. The park he is referencing is beautiful, serene, and has little quaint seating areas everywhere, but it isn't what I'd call *dog friendly.* In fact, I think it's one of the few places in the Pacific Northwest that we can't take our dogs to, as it seems there are more places we can than can't.

He declines my suggestion. "It won't take long. Let's go to the Bark Park another day."

I try not to analyze every word for which way his opinion is swaying. "Okay, that will work. Shall I go right when I'm off? I can probably leave here at 4…"

It is sounding more and more urgent, and if I didn't know what it is about, I'd leave work right now to find out. But it is going to be about whether or not he wants children. Honestly, my feelings have only grown stronger on the subject. But I have no loss of feelings towards Mitchell. As we agree to meet at 4:15, I look at his picture on my computer desktop. He's gorgeous to me, inside and out. I picture the child we could have together. Even though we are both blonde, I envision having a red-haired little girl with fiery blue eyes.

". . .Alright, I'm looking forward to seeing you, Mitchell. I love you."

I hope my words don't have a twinge of desperation, as I now feel the relationship could be on rockier ground than I ever intended, but he said it back and then we ended the call. I say a prayer.

"Dear Lord,

I pray for Your will for my life. I pray for Your strength to wash over me. I pray for Your supernatural peace to let me know whatever happens later, it will be okay. I only want the path You've laid out for me. Help me see the way that I need to go, Lord.

In your name,

Amen."

The workday picks up as I process an approved application for Big Orange, the cat that nearly beats up Katie's mom. I instinctively reach for my phone to text her before I remember she's on her honeymoon, and anything I have to say can wait for her return. I picture her and Eli drinking hot chocolate in a snowy landscape and laugh at the thought of her learning to ski.

My shift ends, and I am at the park at 4:05. Mitchell is thankfully already there, too.

"Samantha." Mitchell waves me over to a darling table for two, and he brings me a Chamomile tea from my favorite coffee shop. He is dressed very nicely in a bright white polo shirt that is buttoned all the way to the top.

What I felt was going to be a breakup, now I am feeling the opposite about. Is he going to propose? That would mean he does want children. And I would say yes in a heartbeat!

"Yes, Mitchell?" I straighten out my blouse, taking a quick glance at my hands. They don't look atrocious, but my polish could be fresher. Oh well. I know my hair is right, as I checked it in the car mirror.

"Thanks for meeting me here today."

I look around the beautiful park. It is quite an idyllic setting after all. We aren't the only ones here, but less than a handful of people are scattered around and not nearby.

"Our relationship has been amazing. You are the perfect woman, Samantha."

Oh yes, this is definitely happening. This is my dream. Thank you, Lord!

"I've given a lot of thought to our conversation about our future, and the possibility of a family. And I take this all very, very seriously. I want you to know that, and I know I've told you this before, but I don't date just to date. I either see a future with someone or I'm not interested."

"And that's what I love about you." I put my hands on his, feeling the slightest hesitation in return.

"Thank you, Samantha. But this is the reason why I am ending things with you today. I do not have the calling or desire for children in the future. While I don't intend on being a bachelor forever because of this, if I am, then that's God's will for my life. I'm sorry, Samantha, and I wish for nothing more than meeting you in the middle of this. I wish there was a way I could fulfill your wants and desires for kids, but I am not able to do so. I feel too strongly otherwise."

My soul knew this was coming, and God prepared me for the heartbreak, but the devastation is creeping in. I try my best to hold it together while we say our goodbyes.

"Thank you for being a wonderful boyfriend to me. I will never forget you, Mitchell." I slide the promise ring off my finger and hold it up for him to retrieve.

He waves it off. "Keep it, Samantha. I want you to have it."

I shake my head. "You knew this ring was going to be special one day, and I want you to give it to your future wife. I mean it. Take the ring, Mitchell."

He hesitates and gently accepts the ring out of my hand. He turns away and walks to his car and leaves. I wander for a few moments, feeling the gaping void of the breakup fully, tears rolling down my cheeks without abandon. Katie is coming home soon, and I will text her the news when I know she's back and settled. I've really missed chatting with her this week since she's been away, and I can't wait to hear all about her honeymoon. But for now, I need a friend to share this heartbreak with.

Chapter 18
Puppy Love & Fresh Powder
Katie

Back in the room, I opened my suitcase again to find my ski outfit. The gorgeous, quilted boots are sitting on top, still unworn, but I am concerned about traipsing through the snow in them, as the height makes them seem like indoor boots—as in wearing for a photo indoors, because wearing them in any appropriate climate outdoors is nearly guaranteed for injury. Unless you are trying to secure a "Slip N' Fall" lawsuit.

"This is Rhonda Meyers reporting from KA2 news, and I'm on location tonight, very, very far away from home. That's right, I'm

coming to you live from Alaska. I'm standing here with Katie Skatey, who I'd like to start off by congratulating on her recent wedding. Katie, what on earth went through your mind when you met the man of your dreams and found out his last name rhymes with yours?"

"   Thank you, Rhonda. I am extremely excited. And truthfully, I think it's kind of cute."

Rhonda nods into the camera. "Well, there you have it, folks."

The camera man whispers something about the topic at hand.

"Right, right. I am here tonight not to discuss the rap that is now this woman's legal name, but the Slip N' Fall case she has filed over Mother Nature. Katie, will you elaborate?"

She holds the microphone to me, and I try to take it, but I realize too late she didn't mean for me to, and we go back and forth for a moment before she relents.

"That's right, Rhonda. You see, I've just been given these gorgeous 'boots' from Norlands, a term applied liberally—shout out to Audrey Fitzgerald for all of your personal shopping needs—and Mother Nature was negligent in the decision to coat the grounds with too much of this white stuff. Woman to woman, Rhonda, we know shoes like these are mostly for show. They aren't intended to be in any weather or elements that aren't a brisk fall day on a solid concrete slab. So, you see, I find this recent accumulation of fresh powder intentional. And the double axel I did whilst stepping outside *this afternoon has not only bruised my ego, but caused much emotional distress, not to mention something else."*

"And just what is that something, Katie?" Rhonda is leaning into the microphone I hold to talk, and I don't want to say it on air, so I whisper it in her ear, not realizing she is slightly hard of hearing.

"You WHAT in your pants? Oh dear."

She does a "cut" motion with her hands to have the camera stop rolling, but she couldn't have been more wrong.

"No! I said I SPLIT my pants!"

Laughter erupts as my voice carries all the way to Florida, but it is too late; the camera is off.

I shudder at the thought of hurting myself and decide I'll pull these boots on for a romantic dinner in the lodge. I pull out the snowsuit that Audrey has packed for me. It is a very pretty mint green and has matching gloves. Eli said that the hotel gave out helmets for us to wear, so I wouldn't need to bring the hat. *Great,* I think. Helmet hair is just what I want to don on my honeymoon. But then again, many activities I've tried should have required a helmet but didn't. In fact, I find it odd just how socially unacceptable helmet wearing can be. What's it to a stranger if I want to protect my head from a tennis ball on the courts? Does it really matter that I'm a bystander, watching the game and not playing? It shouldn't.

I dress in an extra layer of warmth underneath the snowsuit and sheepishly put on a dab of makeup. Just because I'm in the wilderness of Alaska, do I really need to give up my appearance? I'm not sure, and while it seems like I should, I put the makeup on anyway.

Eli returns to the room with two ski passes he acquired from the front desk. "Okay, Mrs. Skatey. Are you ready for a real adventure?"

My mind goes entirely blank, but I feel myself nodding in agreement. "Let's go, Mr. Skatey."

The morning sun peeks over the mountains, casting a golden glow over the Glacier View Lodge as Eli and I step out, bundled up in layers of ski gear. I consider what we are about to embark on: skiing for the first time on our honeymoon? What happened to couples' massages and laying poolside?

Inside the ski rental shop, chaos ensues as we wrangle with our equipment. I struggle to maneuver my feet into the ski boots. Walking in ski boots is unlike anything I've ever experienced. They are heavy, flat, and your foot is essentially immobilized from the shin down. According to the rental shop, if it feels like a bear trap has got your toes, then it's the perfect fit.

"Come on, Katie, it's time to hit the slopes!" Eli exclaims, grabbing my hand and dragging me towards the beginner's area.

As we approach the ski lift, I can't help but feel a sense of dread creeping in. The rickety contraption looks like something straight out of a horror movie, and the thought of dangling high above the ground fills me with an irrational fear.

"Eli, do we have to take the lift?" I plead, clutching onto his arm like a lifeline.

"Yes, but don't worry. It'll be a piece of cake," he insists, leading me towards the line. With a shaky breath, I reluctantly climb onto the lift, gripping onto the safety bar for dear life as we are slowly lifted into the unknown.

A ski instructor sitting with us on the chairlift gives me a quick overview of what to do as he shows us two different foot stances that are named after food.

"When your feet are like this, straight and parallel, it's called 'French fries'." He holds up his skis in the air while I consider how lucky I am to be riding the lift with him. I just wish Eli and I had practiced before we got on the chair, but he was so excited that the moment we were fitted for boots, he pushed me into the chair that took us up the mountain.

The ski patroller goes on about being in 'French fries.' "This is when you just want to *go*. You'll get plenty of speed." He smiles at Eli, who nods in return.

"And what if we want to slow down?" my voice croaked shamefully.

"That's when you do this," he makes a triangle with the tips of his skis almost touching. "It's called 'pizza.' Just don't overdo it, as it kills your knees."

He and Eli get into a conversation about knee injuries while I make both formations on my skis. They are heavy, especially holding them up like I am, but I still make a few attempts as the top is increasingly closer by the moment.

"Have fun, you two." The ski instructor lifts up the bar that covers our laps and holds us securely in the chair while we are still mid-air, causing me to release a blood curdling scream from my chest. He immediately puts his ski poles over my lap and tells me to hold on.

"I'm sorry to scare you, miss. But the bar automatically lifts right there anyway, and you don't want to get tangled up in it."

He makes a motion to the people in a small booth that are operating the lift, and next thing I know, the chair is coming to a complete stop while another person in the red patrol uniform appears to assist me off the chair.

"Well, thank you. What nice service here." I try to regain some sense of dignity, as I tell Eli to go on ahead as I get my bearings, and the instructor says he will show me a few moves.

What I hadn't realized is that we are among the first to ski this morning, and the sun hasn't yet warmed up a big patch of ice right where people disembark. For the average skier, who would casually glide over it, the tips of their skis meet fresh snow nearly instantly. But for a new skier like me, who is over 30 and extremely awkward and without a single athletic bone in her body, it poses quite a hazard; hence, the extra support helping me over the ice.

Eli, having only been skiing in his childhood, picks it back up quite fast and is already practicing his turns while he waits for me to arrive with the instructor, 3 yards away. The man, whose name badge reads *Leighuhm,* tells me to use my poles, but I have no idea what that means. He makes a motion that reminds me of a rowboat, so I pretend my skis are oars on each side of my body. Leighuhm nods, appearing pleased by this.

When we finally make it over to Eli, my arms are sore, and I feel total-body exhaustion. I only realize I am complaining aloud when Leighuhm says it must be the altitude.

I look over at the young gentleman who has been assisting me while my husband sharpens up his ability, that I see now was grossly understate. "Is that the real spelling of your name?"

Leighuhm cackles and rolls his eyes. "Unfortunately, yes. My parents liked the name Liam but wanted an 'unusual' spelling." His use of air quotes reveals to me just how passive- aggressive he feels about his name.

"You can always change it, you know. I work in a law office, and we've had a few of those over the years."

Leighuhm laughs and says something under his breath related to a superhero name and waves me off as he returns to the chairlift to help the next person. I watch for a moment as a child, no older than five, waves their fist at him when he tries to help and expertly glides over the ice, making a small jump at the end.

"Thanks, Leighuhm," I holler back after the little girl so dramatically slighted him, and he waves and wishes us both good luck today.

Leighuhm's name reminds me of a name change case that Chaz took on during my first year at the firm. While it was not required for an attorney to be hired, such as a simple name change case like this, there had been some serious complications when the client tried to proceed without legal help.

It was a day like any other at the firm. I was nose-deep into a law book, searching for answers on the legality of allowing a squirrel to become someone's service animal, when a man stumbled into the office.

"Hi, uhm. . . There was no one at the front desk. Can someone help me?" The desperation on this man's face was palpable.

We all looked past him to our receptionist, who as if on cue, had just returned from the restroom. Thankfully, Chaz stood up.

"I can help ya, bud. Come on over here. What's the issue?"

I smirked as Chaz went into his 'stance': he stood bowlegged, with both his hands in his pockets, whenever he was analyzing a problem.

The man humbly walked over, his hands clasped together as if he was about to thank the academy or get on his knees and plead for help.

"What's your name, bud?" Chaz was a little unprofessional at times, but he was a rather good attorney, so I was glad he was helping this guy.

"That's why I'm here." He lowered his voice to the point we were all craning our necks to hear. Darren even stood up. "It's Snicker."

Chaz, who happened to be a touch hard of hearing thanks to a Fourth of July bottle rocket gone wrong at a summer work barbecue, asked the man to repeat it.

"Snicker."

"Snickers? As in the candy bar?"

The man pulled out his driver's license and shook his head.

"Sir, my name is Snicker *Doodle*."

Chaz gaped at the man's identification. "I see. Gee, I'm sorry about that. But you can petition for a name change without a lawyer."

Mr. Doodle nodded but went on into a lengthy explanation why he needed assistance. It was a long-winded tale involving a cookie maker who's decided to copyright this poor guy's name and wanted to sue him if he didn't for intellectual property.

"That's not how copyright law works. No one is selling you as a product."

The man again sneered. "Except I've been signed to be the spokesperson for a national cookie company that rivals the man trying to sue me. Sir, I need your help to change my name, transfer all my documents, and protect me from this man who is trying to ruin my life."

Chaz nodded, understanding there was a little more going on than what he originally assumed. "Sure, let's go into the conference room and you can walk me through it, okay?"

"Thank you." Snicker Doodle pulled out a file that he brought in with him in his backpack. "I have everything here." Chaz took the file and nodded to Jenna to come and assist him.

The two men talked while walking to the conference room, while Jenna towed behind. "So, what name do you want in exchange?"

"Chocolate Chip."

Chaz laughed, and they went into the room. Jenna winked at me, no doubt trying to hold back her laughter. Darren made a call down the block to the local bakery, with a sudden craving for a sweet treat. Chaz, in the conference room, wasted no time hooking up his laptop. He was standing under the large television screen where he cast an image of a cookie, in his wide stance, listening as Snicker Doodle appeared to be going on and on in his explanation.

Chaz's stance would often become an issue when whatever problem he was analyzing was happening at the water cooler, as the hallway there was quite narrow. Once, Suzie, the self-proclaimed *'Crazy Cat Lady'* tripped on Chaz's heel as she tried to step around him. Once she got up, Chaz smiled, and she thought he was laughing at her, but as we've all learned, he's not that big of a jerk and actually quite sensitive. But it was too late, Suzie snapped at him.

"What—did you just dismount from a horse, Chaz? There's not enough room for both of us in this hallway. I got places to be, so I need you to waddle outta here!"

Chaz's eyes got wide, and along with the rest of the office, grew silent as most run-ins with Suzie ended. She was a great co-worker when it came to reliability and work-ethic, but she was easily triggered. Thankfully, we knew just what to do to calm her down once she got riled up.

"I'm so sorry, Suzie. Truly."

Suzie nodded, slowly softening as she accepted Chaz's apology, so he took the opening to smooth things over.

"Say, did I show you a recent snap of Reginald? Over the weekend, we went to Broadway Lover's festival, and Reginald dressed up as Alexander Hamilton."

Suzie instantly sprung to look and gushed over the photos he held out on his phone, as we all returned to our tasks at hand.

The mention of my work gives me a warm feeling in my heart. I really did enjoy the job, my coworkers, and my boss, Frank. As I follow Eli's effortless glide to where the run begins, in a very awkward shimmy, I wonder where we will end up even at the end of this year.

"Dear Jesus,
Thank You for sending me on this adventure with my new husband.
I pray that the right doors will open for us,

And that wherever we end up in our lives,
May it be Your will.
Amen.
P.S. Please help me not break my neck."

When I feel at peace with the Holy Spirit and the calmness of the Lord washes over me, I open my eyes to where I had been standing in place while people whizzed around me. Eli is used to my moments by now, where I will "freeze in time," as he calls it, and he knows I will often stop what I am doing when I feel overwhelmed and pray. He finds the habit inspiring and, too, started doing it, just in a less chaotic place as I see him standing closer to a tree than any skier would dare get nearby.

"Come closer to me, Katie, so you don't get run over."

I follow his instructions, but since he is to the left and uphill of me, I can't figure out how to do it. He shows me a few steps of walking sideways on the skis, which I try, but end up falling. It isn't a fast fall, though. It is one of those falls that happens in slow motion, where you think the *fall-ee* is going to catch themselves, so onlookers aren't too concerned, but invested enough to watch. When I finally do touch down, it feels like my body is met with a soft, fluffy ice-cold cloud that instantly makes my eyes water and mascara will likely be running down the creases of my face. Eli laughs, helping me up as it takes so long to fall, he makes it in time.

The mountain looks impossibly steep, and yet when other skiers disembark for the bottom, they don't vanish immediately into the angle. I decide the top of the run is a trick to the eyes and just feels like it is a cliff, so I follow Eli's lead as he starts in front of me. When he effortlessly glides, his feet parallel in their motion and no stress to his composure, I mimic his exact movements and very slowly, I do get to the other side of the mountain where he wants me to be.

"That was wonderful, Katie! Now let's just keep making wide turns like that until we get down, okay?"

So, he makes another turn, and I follow. Feeling proud of myself, I am beginning to think I'll finally find a sport I can do, when suddenly, a group of those children who are definitely *not* playing some wild game of Red Rover come down the mountain at a greater speed than I could ever anticipate.

"Katie, watch out!"

The children begin barreling into me, as their hands never unlink in their fast descent. I fall to my side, head pointed downward, but Eli is quick to grab a hold of me so I won't slide anywhere. Moments later (and much too late), the ski patroller Leighuhm reemerges.

"Yikes, uh, so sorry about this. I told the kids to wait for me at the top."

The children are all laughing, wearing brightly colored bibs reading *SkiSkool* on the front, *as if the 'Student Driver' bumper sticker ever really helped anyone?* I'd personally rather not know if the person riding my bumper is behind the wheel for the first time or the thousandth. Can we assume that unless the car has a sticker that states, *"Hit me, I need the money,"* we should try our hardest to avoid any collision?

After everyone is checked and cleared for injuries, Leighuhm goes down the mountain with the kids in tow. They never once break their hand holding chain, even when they crash. I'm not sure if I find it admirable or should be concerned that their hands are glued together.

"You ready?" Eli grins at me, and through his reflected ski goggles, I see myself. I look quite sporty and confident, so I realize it is time to act like it, too.

"Yes. Go ahead, I'll be right behind you." For just a moment, instead of looking down, I look ahead and marvel at the beauty of God's creation, feeling instantly grounded as I remember that the God who made these snow-capped mountains that sparkled in the sunlight, put me here in this moment to enjoy it. And the moment I really take it all in, Eli zooms past me, letting out a low howl of enjoyment.

"Eli, wait for me!" I shout, attempting to follow suit.

I know he is using his best reverse psychology on me, and it works; I don't even hesitate to start down the slope. But my attempts at grace and elegance are quickly thwarted as I careen down the slope like a runaway train after the speed comes on much too suddenly for my comfort. My limbs are flailing as I try everything to slow myself down. My sudden downhill speed is gaining traction and feels like any moment, I will implode. It is then I remember to do the 'pizza' stance that Leighuhm showed me, when I come to a sudden halt and topple over, falling backwards.

Eli, now skiing uphill to me, is trying his hardest not to laugh. He reaches down to me, attempting to pull me back up to standing, when I forget my legs are attached to waxed metal sticks, and I slide right back down again. It is at this point he can no longer contain his fit of laughter.

"Katie, you're a natural!" he calls out between hysterical fits. "I'm seriously *so impressed*." He is choking the words out while I lay there, starting to see the humor in the situation myself, and joining in. As far as I can tell, I'm not injured anywhere, I'm not crying, and I can bet my eyebrows are still intact.

After several hours of skiing, I am feeling pretty confident that I have set a new beginner's record of going down the mountain in under three hours. It may have just been the one time, and while I'm not familiar with ski areas, that is a very challenging run for beginners. Eli isn't so sure, but he entertains the idea with me that it is in fact, impressive. Sure, he had to coax me down the first time with extra marshmallows on my hot chocolate that would be waiting for us to order in the lodge. The rest of the way down was not easy, and when the children had gone by for the third time, I was feeling weak and unsure of my footing. Let's just say, they have very kind drivers of the snowcat, and I appreciate their willingness to take me the rest of the way down. I only had to wait for an hour, which in hindsight seems very reasonable. From what I understand, the ride is normally reserved for the injured, but thanks to my donation made to the mountain Search and Rescue, they are willing to take me.

*****

The remaining days of our trip are filled with what I had pictured all along: snow angels, romantic picnics, and the type of adventure you only find while in a new place. The hotel has not one but two hot tubs, so we are excited for a dip at the end of each day, while thankfully, my bathing suit still fits despite all of the excess desserts.

We think we successfully time our soak for right after the dinner rush, as neither of us believe in the old wives' tale of getting cramps after eating. And we are elated that we find both hot tubs empty. But when we finally submerge in the water, three people join us shortly after. Eli looks over at me and smirks. Out of the two hot tubs—did they have to choose ours?

The small group seems like my mother's kind of people, because the entire time we are sharing the bubbling waters with them, they are talking about cases. After a few minutes, we hear something that catches our ears.

"No, that's not what *Mystery Maven* said. She believes that Kyle is just the fall guy, remember? I agree with her."

I look at Eli, and we both let out a silent laugh.

The group thinks we are laughing at them, so I quickly jump into the backpedal. "My mother is . . . um... she's *Mystery Maven.*"

The wide gaped expressions from the three people are in perfect unison.

"Is she OKAY?"

All three people are rambling off questions, but this one I am especially hung up on.

"What do you mean?" I stand up in the hot tub, my upper body freezing solid, but I am extremely concerned.
"They arrested Corky Meyers at her location. You remember, the costumed hot dog guy? I guess he was stalking her!"

My hands cover my mouth, and Eli and I both rush out of the tub, frantically putting on our hotel robes. I think back to our conversation earlier. Everything was fine. Of course, we had just been texting, as she encouraged me not to call, that everything and the dogs were doing wonderful. Now I feel like such a chump.

Once we are able to successfully put on the oversized robes—*how can something have so much fabric and yet the belt is so short*—we run to the elevator and make our way to the room, grabbing our phones immediately. I call my mother, except she doesn't answer on the first ring, and with every passing second, my stomach flips.

On the fourth ring, a breathless voice comes on the other line. "Katie?"

My mother, always questioning if it's really me or a captor.

"Mom! We just heard that Corky—".

She cuts me off. "I'm okay, and the dogs are okay, don't worry." My mother sounds like she is outside.

"Where are you? What happened?" I demand answers, feeling concerned that she went through something scary, putting the call on speakerphone so Eli can hear in real time.

"We are at the Bark Park, and I'm with Marge. We are all safe now. There was a little panic this morning as I took Dolly and Carter on our daily trip to the doggy bakery to get their dozen treats from grandma, when there was a man dressed up as a cat sitting outside on the bench. Normally, I wouldn't have thought a thing of it, but Dolly and Carter went nuts. They barked at the person from the moment we pulled up in the parking lot. They actually barked off some serious calories, so don't worry about their weight gain, though, they *might* need to go on Jenny Craig. Anyway, we were sitting in the car still, as none of us liked the look of that costume, when suddenly, the cat came towards me. On all fours, Katie! It was frightening. Then, when it reached the car, I opened the door as hard as I could, knocking him out. Thankfully, an FBI detective was nearby picking up from the bakery and saw the whole thing. He came out and tore off the cat mask. It was my stalker, Corky Meyers!"

Eli and I look at each other with concern as my mother recounts a frightening run in. "We are so glad you are safe. I can't believe that he came out there, several states away! How did he know you were there?”

“That is a good question, but my listeners believe that his costume maker sold me out. You’ll never guess who it is.”

As if on cue, we all say the same name. “Trisha Pawsbury!” The woman who’s been buying my doggy creations to resell in her boutique. I should’ve known better than to ever use my personal address on a return envelope, prison pen pal or otherwise.

“Why would she do that to me?” I wonder aloud. Sure, I had told her about my wedding and honeymoon trip, and I recalled her asking about my setup for the dogs while I was away.

“I’m sorry, I think I did mention to her that you were coming to stay. I just can’t believe she would share all of my information like that with just anyone.” I feel betrayed by Trisha, but thankful that everyone is okay.

“If it makes you feel any better, Katie, I don’t think Trisha told him anything. Her store was ransacked about two weeks ago, and her address book was stolen. It was in her notes that you were going away, you see. She may have mentioned something to her old pal, Corky, but he still broke in to get the personal information.”

That did make me feel slightly better, but I still want to hear Trisha’s side of the story when I return and decide if I will still be doing business with this woman.

After the rest of our debriefing, we say our goodbyes on the phone, and she promises to send over some more photos. She reminds us that she will be retrieving us from the airport and to enjoy our last night in Alaska.

She makes quick on her promise of more photos and sends a handful over the moment we hang up the phone. Dolly and Carter at PetWorld, in the shopping cart with Mitchell pushing it; next, the dogs are wearing chef's clothes and making paw print cookies at the dog bakery. Eli and I are howling in laughter at each photo that we treasure. The next picture is of dog food bowls that look like they have been monogrammed with the dogs' initials. It warms our hearts as we talk about how we can't wait to see them again, and we go to the next picture: Dolly and Carter wearing police uniforms as Corky sits in the back seat of a police car, wearing cat ears. I am a little worried about that one, as he could be dangerous for all we know, but at least he was detained when my mother randomly held a photoshoot with police uniforms she just happened to have on hand.

"Where does she come up with this stuff?"

Eli's question makes me relieved. I know my mother can be a bit much. Okay, a bit more than much. An enormous amount of much... But she's my mother, and I am once again reminded just how good the Lord was in his match for Eli and me. He's my person, and for that, I am forever thankful.

I put the phone down, knowing that my mother is safe, the dogs are being spoiled to the point they need a weight loss program, and tomorrow we will leave our Alaskan wonderland to return home and start our forever together.

"Shall we dress and go get that special 'Baked Alaska' dessert one more time?" Eli asks me with wonder in his eyes. I told him I enjoyed it, but it was he who was truly obsessed.

"You don't think they will let you order it for breakfast tomorrow?" I give him a wink. "And yes, that sounds like a lovely treat. Maybe we can figure out how to make that at home."

We have a long talk while we eat dessert and have tea over what waits for us when we return.

"I don't want to sour the mood, but I'm feeling a little anxious about what's going to happen when we go home." Eli speaks from the heart as I listen.

"I know you said you were willing to move, but you love your job, and your co-workers are a blast. I just want you to tell me if you want to stay where we are. If so, I will do whatever I have to, to make it work. I'll even change professions."

"But you love the foot!" I laugh as he nods and smiles. I continue. "I have given it a lot of thought. I know I'm blessed with a good work environment, and of course we love our church families, but I am ready for a new adventure. In our market, it would take us eons to be able to buy a house. I don't want that; I'd love for the doggies to have a yard. And truthfully, I wouldn't mind escaping the rain."

"How did I get so lucky?" Eli leans in for a passionate kiss.

We pay the bill and walk back to our room, hand in hand.

"There's something else." Eli speaks softly, turning to me. He looks like he has a confession to make, and I'm not sure if it is going to be good or bad by the looks of it.

"It's not just the job opportunities that make me want to move to another state. There is something to which I've always been drawn. Whenever I see it or even hear about it, I get butterflies. And I've just looked up a few clubs for it, and they have a hub of sorts, out west."

He has my full attention, but as we stand looking at each other in the hotel lobby, the elevator dings, and we step inside.

"Well? What is it?" My mind races in wonder as I consider just what this hobby is that he hasn't shared with me until after we've signed a legal document.

"Dear Jesus,
Please don't let Eli's interest involve underwater basket weaving.
In your name,
Amen."

Eli shuffles around before telling me. "It sounds silly, but. . . I've always wanted to be involved in dog shows."

I let out a laugh of relief and tell him that sounds amazing. "Do you picture you and Carter competing?"

"Well, yes, but I'd want to be involved in a special show just for rescue dogs. I admit, I know very little about the production side of things, but for dogs like Carter and Dolly who don't necessarily have AKC papers but want to compete, or for dogs who aren't physically perfect but physically able. . . Wouldn't it be amazing to have a show just for them? I was thinking something like, "Tails of Triumph" or "Second Chance Showcase." We could have it be a multi-day event where dog rescuers could come in with their adoptable animals, pet food companies would sponsor, and makers like yourself could even sell your creations. I'd call it the "Rescue Round Up." Very western, don't you think? I mean, when in Rome. . ."

"I absolutely love it! All of it. Why haven't you told me any of this before? You know I will support any of your ideas, as long as they don't involve clowns, hula hoops, or joining the circus in any of its forms."

"Well, I wanted to tell you, but didn't want to put any pressure on you with the idea of moving. It's already stressful enough of a prospect to then have the pressure of just how excited I am for it. I guess what I'm trying to say is. . . I want your dreams to come true, too, Katie. Your happiness is my happiness. We are in this together and if anything —and I mean anything—in this life we have together suddenly doesn't jive or you don't like the idea from the start, I want you to be completely honest with me. I love our plans and now that I know you're on board with moving and it doesn't worry you or cause anguish, that's when I knew it was time to share with you about my idea for the dog shows."

The more I think about the dog shows this evening, the more it makes sense. We even dream about a venue that could hold my handmade dog fashions. With our mutual agreement that we will have better opportunities elsewhere, there is just one more thing we need to do. We close our eyes, and we pray. Out loud and together. For our future, for our hopes and dreams, for the things that we aren't sure about, and for our family and friends. We don't want to lose any of the friendships we've made. Eli wants to make sure the right person will take over his youth group and Bark Park ministry, and I want to make a pact that we try and visit at least once a year.

"My parents are going to be visiting so frequently that we will need at least a three bedroom." Eli laughs as we crawl into bed, depleted from the wonderful trip. He set the alarm on his phone so that we can wake up with enough time to have a leisurely breakfast before heading to the airport.

"Why a three bedroom? Unless the dogs are finally getting that playroom you've been promising them." I chuckle.

"A three bedroom because you and I both know that your mother will already be staying in the guest bedroom as often as possible."

We both laugh ourselves silly considering the scenarios of our families intertwining in the future.

"Did you know our dads are going to racquetball camp?" Eli asks me.

"What now? Like a sleepaway camp?" The image of our dads sharing a canoe and roasting marshmallows around a campfire comes into my mind.

"Pretty much, except they are staying nearby at a hotel. They are going to get trained by a retired player named Sam Sanderson. Guess he was famous back in the day. At least to the level that he can charge $500 per person for a week of training."

Eli tells me more details about the camp, which my father will be flying back for next month, and then they will drive two hours south together for the training camp.

We are yawning pretty hard at this point, and both start to doze off. It takes everything I have to turn off the lights.

While the honeymoon has been amazing, full of adventure and memories we will never forget, I am most looking forward to returning to the calm realities of life. Traveling is a blast, and I know that it is important to Eli, so I will look forward to a lifetime of fun getaways. But for me, true love is shared every day of the year. I will get just as much joy out of watching a movie with him and the dogs on the couch as eating in a fancy restaurant here at the resort. I look forward to making his birthday cakes, eating the lunches he packs for me, or mailing out Christmas cards with our family portraits. I will support him emotionally while he looks for another job, and wherever we may end up with that. True love is not just the good times, but it's in the quiet and mundane Tuesdays of life.

The hustle and bustle of the airport, even in a small town in Alaska, is apparent in the morning. It must be because it's the weekend, and people are dying to get out. Judging by the family standing in line ahead of us to go through airport security, they are going somewhere warm and tropical. Or they just dress really poorly for the weather in Alaska.

A short woman taps on my shoulder, and I spin around. She has sweat in her brow as she asks if she can go in front of us.

"I—I am so sorry to ask, but I overslept this morning, and now my flight is already boarding. If I miss the flight, I'll never know whether or not I was seated next to my future husband. Can you imagine? I came here for a work trip, not meeting any of these single men that supposedly exist three to one woman, and I miss my chance on the way home? What if I get bumped to a later flight and sit next to a nun? Was this trip all in vain?"

"Good luck." I wave her off to go through security first. It's a small airport, and thankfully there are two lines she can choose from, but Eli and I both cringe as she chooses the longer of the two. As we get ushered over to go through security next, we are told we need to remove our shoes, jacket, hats, jewelry, belts, and cargo pants, if applicable. Unfortunately, that lists just about everything I am wearing. With one look in my direction, a TSA agent says I can have a private screening behind a flimsy cubicle they have set up next to the x-ray machine.

Once we make it past security, we stop at a small gift shop to pick up our souvenirs. "We should've thought of this while we were at the hotel. Now we are probably paying double for our magnets, tree ornaments, and chocolate candies that are reminiscent of... moose poop?" I pick up the bag that Eli had sat on the counter on top of a new collection of tie-dye shirts. When I laugh at his love of the pattern, he winks.

"I got you a matching one, so now my favorite person will be wearing my favorite pattern."

I browse the pet section to see if there is anything we can take the dogs, while Eli looks for something for our parents.

"What do you think about these for your mother?" Eli holds up what looks like two giant King Salmon, and upon further inspection, I realize they are life-like slippers. "I also found this book about unsolved mysteries of Alaska."

"How do you know her so well?" I am so pleased. "Remind me to have you do our Christmas shopping!"

"Find anything for the furbabies?" he asks with a twinkle in his eye. He is just as excited about reuniting with them as I am.

I hold up two sets of dog slippers that look like bear paws and pajamas that button up around the behind, with a small opening for their tails. "Could these get any cuter?"

"Oh my word. Don't forget Edward; he's going to want the same outfit." Eli is totally right, and I grab one more of each.

When we finally board the plane, the short woman from earlier that had cut us in line to be a few moments faster is on our flight. She begrudgingly walks down the aisle of the plane, where we sit squarely in the center left side, with one open seat next to us. Of course, her seat is that one.

"Hello, again. I missed my flight, so it's safe to say, prince charming will not be on this flight, and I'll be single *forever.*" The woman giggles, in which, we join her, kindly.

I know all too well the feeling of loneliness and wanting to find a partner. We begin to ask her a few questions about her life as we wait for the last passengers to shuffle in. She tells us she is a junior partner at a law firm out west and has to come out to visit one of the retiring partners to help him with some in-person legal matters. No one else wanted to come, so she willingly volunteered.

"What a coincidence. I am a paralegal at a firm in the Northwest." I share just a snippet, not knowing how interested she will be, but she jumps on the information eagerly. We end up telling her about our impending move, the dogs, and Eli's work. All of this transpires in just a few minutes when we finally hear the plane door close. A flight attendant comes over to the intercom and thanks us for our patience.

"Good morning, Alaska travelers. Thank you for waiting for us this morning. We were alerted there was one passenger who missed the morning flight and only just arrived. We thought we'd allow him to board the plane by giving him an extra moment of grace."

We all look up with high hopes as the woman next to us, who's name we had just learned is Kara, audibly gasps. The man has slicked back hair and is wearing bright red plaid and new blue jeans with big black boots. He looks like a lumberjack cliche, square jaw and all. It happens in slow motion as the only seat available is across the aisle from us, and when he sits down, Kara wastes no time.

"Kara Peters," she holds out her beautifully manicured, slender hand.

He smiles ear to ear and returns her gesture with a burly hand. "Kevin James, nice to meet you."

Someone behind us smirks, and Kara looks utterly disappointed, but she doesn't seem completely put off. He may have inhaled the helium from a balloon right before entering the plane for all I know, but likely not. Kevin's high voice rivals the glass breaking pitch of an opera singer.

"It's like they say," I whisper to Kara, who is now facing forward. "The odds are good, but the goods are odd."

After takeoff, Kevin seems extremely interested in talking to Kara, who is now flat out ignoring him. Eli and I try to stay out of it, but it is really funny to watch.

"Is it just his voice? Or something else?" I speak in a low tone when thankfully, Kevin gets up to use the bathroom, and the moment he does, Eli looks over.

"It could grow on you. We are stuck on this plane for three hours. Is it really that bad? We only heard him say his name. Maybe he was just nervous meeting you, and his voice spiked."

I cock an eyebrow at Eli, not realizing he is such a matchmaker.

"I suppose I could give him another chance to speak. What if it's intolerable? He is exactly the type of man I picture when I think of my future husband. And when I saw him, I felt love at first sight."

Her dramatics are familiar to me, having been in the same situation not long ago. When you're single for longer than you expect to be, every chance meeting becomes something more.

We know she is coming around to the idea as he sits back down and attaches his seatbelt. "So, Kevin. Do you live in Alaska?"

His voice is as high as we remembered, but after some time of him speaking, it seems to soften a little. He even brings it up.

"I know my voice is different. My vocal chords were injured in a hockey game. I am actually traveling to get a consultation on their repair."

You can see the regret flash across Kara's face as he explains in depth his injury.

"They don't believe they can fix it, but there is this new treatment that I am allowed to try. It's still experimental and all but imagine like an antidote to helium. It's something that you inhale that drops your voice down to a normal level. I'd settle for anything lower than this, of course."

"So, is it like an inhaler?"

As Kara and Kevin bounce back and forth in conversation, the whole plane is quiet and listening in. Someone even shushes another passenger as he goes on about the treatment.

"Sort of. It's a weird mist, so I guess it's more akin to vaping? Hard to say until I see it, but it comes in a little handheld device." He just literally describes vaping in a roundabout way. "Long list of side effects, though." He runs his burly hand over his black hair that is shined up and combed back.

"Oh yeah? Like what? I mean if you don't mind me asking."

My mind immediately flashes back to that press-on veneers commercial I saw a few weeks ago.

"Baldness and loss of muscle mass, for starters."

Kara's face falls, as she returns looking forward. Her mouth is in a full-blown pout as she weighs the options.

"Is there a hidden camera in here?" Eli whispers to me, laughing in disbelief.

"Are there any risks of leaving your voice as-is?" Someone from the back of the plane shouts out to Kevin. Kara, just realizing that the entire plane has been listening in on their conversation, blushes and puts her feet up on her seat, wrapping her arms around her legs.

"No. The damage is already done but won't progress from here. Thank you for your question. Anyone else?"

Kevin is now standing up, facing towards the back of the plane and calling on people who have their hand in the air like this is elementary school.

"It was a freak accident. A sports injury involving a hockey puck to my throat."

"Are you coming around to Kevin?" I whisper to Kara, who looks over at Eli and me and smiles.

"I guess it's not as bad as I originally thought." She smiles, sheepishly.

I am so glad Kara feels that way, because to me, it seems even higher. Just then, an equally high, squeaky voice belonging to a woman pipes up in the back.

"Hi, Kevin. I just want to say I know how you feel with your voice. Living with an unbelievable soprano in your throat isn't easy. But there is an upside: You will always be able to find work in a children's choir."

A few snickers and cheers echo through the plane, and the flight attendant comes through with drinks. I am expecting a bag of miniature salted peanuts that has to be shelled from a dwarf plant type that they only grow in airplane snack farms, but instead, she gives me a brittle cookie that crumbles all over my clothes the moment I bite into it and also down my windpipes, sending me into a coughing frenzy. Eli gives me some water to wash it down with, but for a moment when I thank him, my voice squeaks just as high as Kevin's. We look at each other with wide eyes, as surely, he thinks we are mocking him.

Kara and Kevin end up exchanging phone numbers. He is going to be staying in the city, where she has a layover, so she agrees to have lunch with him when they land.

"Eli, Katie, do you have time to join us for lunch?" Kara asks as the plane lands.

As much as we would enjoy it, we are exhausted, and my mother is likely already here waiting for us.

"Ahh, I'm afraid not. Our ride is probably already here."

She nods understandably and brings up our move again.

"Look, I know it's a long shot, but since you don't know where you're moving to yet," Kara is wrestling with a zipper when she reaches into her purse, retrieving a business card. . . "Katie, give me a call if you ever come out west and need a job. You seem like an awesome woman, and I could put in a good word for you at our firm."

"Thank you, Kara! That is so kind of you. It has been lovely meeting you, and of course, good luck with Kevin."

She motions to the business card I hold in my hand.

"My cell is on the back. Text me yours, and I'll keep you in the loop." She winks at us and quickly vanishes into the sea of people disembarking the airplane into a crowded corridor.

It is always a mad dash to get off of a plane. People stand immediately, before the door even opens and most of the time will still wait for people to leave, row by row, before exiting themselves, unless they are particularly stealthy and can slip out. It reminds me of elementary school. When the bell rang for recess, we'd break out in the race of our lives to the twirling bars, but the littlest girl in our class, Annabelle, would always make it there first.

When we get off the plane, Eli and I let out a collective sigh of relief.

"Well... *that was a trip of a lifetime,*" I whisper to him, feeling the exhaustion finally set in. He, too yawns, nodding in agreement.

"Tell me about it. If this is what marriage is, why didn't we do it sooner?" He winks.

"How much sooner could we have married? I suppose you could've gotten down on one knee the day we met, but I'd still have needed at least a week to prepare." I look at him smartly.

"My knee would've squished down in the landmine you stepped in, so at least I could have saved you the embarrassment!"

My face reddens in embarrassment. "You said you didn't see that!" I tug on his hair playfully, and he gives me a kiss on the cheek.

A traffic jam in the terminal stops us up. Two golf carts that transport the elderly and the oversleeping collide. No one is injured, but an ice coffee is spilled, and in the legal world, it's about the same thing.

We slowly make our way through the crowd to the luggage carousel, where my mother will be waiting for us.

"Do you see her anywhere?" Eli asks as we ride down the escalators.

"Not yet. . . Oh wait," I turn to him. "Promise me you'll still love me."

"What's that?" He gives a confused look and then turns, frantically searching the crowds with a furrowed brow. "Ha! That woman —where does she come up with this?"

"Katie- Eli! I'm right here!" My mother is waving her right arm in the air, the left arm too busy holding a sign that reads, *"Welcome Back from Prison.'*

"Hi," I quietly call back to her, but everyone who's read her sign looks at me with a very *concerned* look as they pull their purses and luggage a little closer to themselves.

"I'm so glad you made it home safely! The dogs will be so excited. And we have much to catch up on: I've just gotten word that Kyle's men have been detained by the US Marshals and will no longer be a threat to anyone. We can all breathe easy tonight!"

"That's great news," Eli says as he slips his arm over my shoulder, holding me tight.

"Now that you're here, I'll go get the car and bring it around while you wait for your luggage."

"Thanks, that will be great, mom." Eli echoes my words.

Once she steps outside, we relish in a quiet moment while staring at the conveyor belt that hasn't started moving yet. As we wait for our luggage, we stand in silence, with his arm around me. His phone buzzes in his pocket, but he doesn't reach for it.

"I need to savor these last moments before we return to reality." I agree with his sentiment. The luggage comes too quickly, and we go outside to wait after retrieving it.

It isn't but a few minutes later, she comes peeling out around the corner in her rental car, but there is another piece of the puzzle she hasn't clued us in on yet.

"Katie, Eli, this is Garreth. Like Garrett with an H. Garrethhh, Garr-*eth*. Imagine pronouncing an S after your tongue gets stung by a bee."

I always feel guilty in some way for people who come in contact with my mother, but somehow, I still don't know how to feel about Garreth because I am so confused.

"Okay, got it. Who is he?"

"Well, there is another thing I didn't tell you about yet. I didn't want you to freak out since it was your honeymoon and all."

Sweat is forming on my upper lip. The freaking out has arrived, and Eli takes my hand as he can hear the thoughts trying to escape my lips and come blurting out my mouth.

"What's going on?" he politely asks.

"The day before Corky was arrested, there were a few sightings of him. I admit, I got a little freaked out and I called the FBI. I guess Corky had run in some of the same circles with some pretty scary people. Do you remember the news story about the gang who broke into the pigeon rescue and held the workers hostage until they successfully trained the birds to launder money? *Those were his cousins.* So, out of an abundance of caution, they were about to put me in the witness protection program, but I only agreed to it if I could take my entire family with me. How could I leave to start my new life in Wyoming without ever seeing Dolly and Carter again? What would Edward think if he could never play with his cousins? At first, I offered to trade your father for the dogs, but that just didn't feel right considering they are your dogs, too."

"Too? What? Witness protection?

"But don't worry, all of the men have been arrested. Apparently, Corky sold out their location the moment he was denied a litter box down at the station. Now, we just need to check Garreth back in at the bureau. It will be like none of this ever happened."

"Check him back in? Is he a book from the library?"

"Oh, Katie. You have such a sense of humor. He does have day privileges, so he can accompany us for the rest of the afternoon, if we want. We just have to get him back before dinner time. Trust me," she cupped her hand over her mouth, as if that made him go deaf, "you do NOT want to be around this guy when he's hungry!"

"Why is that?" My patient husband asked in wonder.

"He makes those mukbang ASMR videos for a hobby." As my mother goes into the bureau with the agent, before

dropping us off back home, my phone buzzes. "I guess we better check our messages, huh?" I ask Eli. He sighs, nodding as he takes his phone out. I check my texts, happy to see mine are from Samantha.

Hello to my favorite newlywed! I trust your trip was divine. Can we schedule some girl time ASAP? I'm afraid Mitchell and I have broken up, and I'm devastated. I really thought he was the one. (broken heart emoji)

I gasp at Samantha's text and read it aloud to Eli. We are both shocked, confused, and sad.

"They made a wonderful couple. I'm really surprised, but we don't know what happened yet. Let's pray about it and see what kind of guidance we can give them."

Eli's words ring true, and he agrees to reach out to Mitchell first thing tomorrow and set up a time to meet up with them. Instead of replying to Samantha with a generic *"oh no, so sorry"* on the wings of my marital bliss, I will reply to her after much heartfelt thought, because if there's anything I know well, it is loneliness. So, I'll wait until I am alone to reply. I want to get it right for Samantha.

I stretch my legs out as far as I can in the back seat of the car, yawning and leaning my head on Eli's shoulder, and considering the caveat of finding someone to marry. There can be so much hardship in our lives, but once you open yourself up to finding a partner, we have all those horrid feelings of insecurity, awkwardness, shyness, and frumpiness. We try things we normally wouldn't, and when a friend says she met her fiancé at a knife throwing contest, we ignore the red flags and buy a ticket to the next night. Because the most dangerous part of navigating our life is, and always will be, comparison. It is a thief of joy. God doesn't have us all on the same path. How boring would it be if He did? No, we all have the freedoms and varying tastes and ideas to make life extraordinarily different from one another, and that also includes when or if we marry.

Before I met Eli, I admit, I was feeling desperate for a partner. While God had plans for me that I hadn't yet understood, I remained faithful in His timing and continued to wait. But then, after my sweet dog came into my life, I felt whole in a way I hadn't in years. Though my now husband came very soon after, I realize in retrospect, marriage isn't a bandage for feeling complete. It isn't a cure-all for loneliness and longing. The only place that true peace comes from is turning our lives over to Christ.

As if on cue, Eli squeezes my shoulder as he puts his arm around me. "I have quite the interesting message as well."

"Oh? What is it?"

"You know that website I posted my resume on? Well, a clinic just reached out to me and asked if I'd like to interview over Zoom this week. You'll never guess where they are located."

"What—where?" I am about to jump out of my skin with excitement, imagining living in a new place.

"Southern Montana, just an hour from your folks."

The shock drains my face of color. I am overjoyed with the prospect of being so close to my family.

"That sounds amazing. Let's pray about it right away!" And we do while we waited for my mother to return. The Lord will guide our paths, just as He promises if we trust Him to do so. My heart jumps at the thought, and I feel a rush of excitement runs through me as Eli and I have the rest of our lives to look forward to.

Chapter 19
Leashes and Lullabies
Carolyn

"How is everything fitting?" I gently rap on the dressing room door of *Boot Scoot*, the premier western wear outfitter of Wyoming.

"Love the top, but I think I need a bigger size. This baby just isn't giving me any grace here."

Michelle opens the door, revealing a pink paisley top that is stretched to its limits. "Don't worry, I'll get this size, too, for when my baby bearing days are behind me."

We giggle our way through the store as she picks out a handful of other things she wants. "I ain't trying these on. There's only so much I can take. If they don't fit, I'll just save them but pray for me. I have something to wear tonight. It's our last date night before I get induced."

"Congratulations! And I am praying for you every day. Where is Nick taking you tonight?"

I beam, knowing the love she has with her husband. I have, too, with mine, and I can't wait to see him when I get off work.

"He's taking me to the steakhouse for my favorite chicken fried steak, because I'd like to live the rest of this pregnancy as if I'll never want to fit into any of my clothes again. Then, we will be going out for ice cream. It's basically my last weekend of eating with no abandon."

"Well, you are eating for two!" I wink at her and listen as she goes on to tell me all about her baby girl.

"Her name will be Rae Adeline Ford. What do you think?" When she said it, her hand made a bow.

I love the name, gushing over it with her, picturing a beautiful blonde baby that looks just like Michelle but with pink hair bows and sparkle cowgirl booties. The boutique I work at also sells baby clothes, so it is very hard not to think about babies all the time. Micah will tease me that I'm working in an environment that induces baby fever. I will shoot back that we also sell dog accessories, so he has that to worry about, too.

He is the one down at the animal shelter every week volunteering for an hour. They have so many building maintenance issues and can't afford to hire it out, so he will pitch in every Thursday afternoon, when his shift at the firehall is over. Twice, he's called me, wanting my opinion on if the dogs will get along with a big peach cat that has stolen his heart. He will send me pictures of her every time he is in there, even taking the Chihuahuas down to meet her. I tell him to bring her home, but he is worried about the space. We are quickly overgrowing the small cabin at his parents, but it is still more room than the kitty has in her small kennel. He vows to bring her home this weekend when we are both off and can go pick her up. His heart for animals is one of my favorite things about him.

When Katie texted me that afternoon that Eli was considering a job offer just an hour away from us, I couldn't believe it. It is a different world out here, but in the best way. I immediately responded and told them to call me any time if they need help finding a place to stay.

Since Micah and I are now expectant parents, the cabin is shrinking with my expanding waist. We just put an offer in on a house that's just a mile from his parents' ranch. It's a fixer upper that needs a wild amount of work, and with three dogs, a cat, and soon to be baby boy in the mix, I am constantly thinking about the chaos that's soon to unfold with living in a construction zone. We can stay in the cabin until it's livable, thankfully, but part of me loves the chaos. The dogs barking. The cat hissing at the Chihuahuas who just want her love. The baby planning. All of the hustle in our house is just a reminder of the love that two people shared so strongly, they said vows to one another in front of their loved ones and made a promise to never stop working on the marriage. To keep taking care of each other. To never give up. And with God at the center of ours, I know we never will.

Acknowledgements

After I published *A New Leash on Life,* I've had readers ask me if there was going to be more to Katie and Eli's story. Since their fictional lives are so close to my own heart, I was thrilled to find that people wanted to read more, and most importantly, I am not the only one with a silly sense of humor! As I continue this series, I want to thank my readers for your support, and I hope you enjoy where this story is taking them. Stay tuned for more in this series!

Thank you to my editor, Ronda. You make my words readable!

I also want to thank my mother, who continues to provide non-stop inspiration for her book character, Mystery Maven. May you always be suspicious, because it sure keeps us laughing.

About the Author

Cassandra discovered her passion for writing at the age of seven when she purchased a diary at the Scholastic Book Fair. What began with journal entries about her school and home life later evolved into a collection of poems, short stories, and novels.

Her hobbies include skiing, traveling around the Rocky Mountains, and reading. Much of her writing inspiration stems from her love of dogs, her Onondaga heritage, and her Christian faith.

Cassandra's favorite genres of books are Christian fiction novels, Thrillers, and anything British.

She is a full-time writer and resides in the mountains of Wyoming with her husband, Chad.

Other Books

A New Leash on Life: A Dog-Mom Rom-Com, Book 1
Get ready for a hilarious Christian romantic comedy as we follow the journey of a thirty-something introverted woman, Katie Fitzgerald, who's longing for a husband. But when she accidentally adopts a dog, she discovers that love comes in unexpected ways, and that God's timing is always perfect.

Genre: Christian Romantic Comedy

The Après-Ski Proposal: A Romcom About Love Off-Piste
She came for a fresh start... Not a fake boyfriend. When Claire Riley gets dumped on the eve of her 30th birthday, she's blindsided. A spur-of-the-moment ski trip seems like the perfect escape, until she runs into her ex... With his new girlfriend. Shocked and desperate for a lifeline, Claire accepts a proposal from a charming stranger to pose as her fake-boyfriend. What begins as a simple act of saving face turns into a journey that reveals a fresh start in life and love—the kind that only God could have planned.
Genre: Christian Romantic Comedy

The Curse of Josephine Bagley

Over the course of a century, three individuals are woven together by a decades-old curse:

William, after surviving an Indian raid on his orphanage due to his facial disfigurement, goes on to live among the tribe. But when misfortune befalls them, he is quickly traded away and faced with a pivotal choice that changes his life forever.

Josephine has faced immense loss. Despite her granddaughter's efforts to help her find solace in faith, she finds she can't let go of the past and falls further into her belief that she's eternally bound to darkness.

Saraphina, a fledgling antiques dealer, gets the surprise of her life when a courier delivers notice that she's the last surviving relative of the Bagley Estate. What seemed like a windfall that could help her career now causes her to question her own reality.

In this tale of intertwining mystery, loss, and faith, these souls navigate through nefarious trials to find the gift of grace and forgiveness that extends to us all.

Genre: Christian Gothic